Caught Off Guard

Clint nodded, and the three of them went out the door. They were halfway down the stairs when the shots started. Clint heard them, then pushed Bethany to the side and hit the ground. He rolled down the steps the rest of the way, banging his left elbow painfully, but producing his gun with his right hand.

He came up on one knee, looking for the shooter or shooters, but they were gone. One barrage was all they had the nerve for.

He looked up the stairs at Appo, who seemed to be in shock. His face was white as a sheet.

"You okay?" Clint asked.

"I think so." Appo patted his body. "I'm—I'm not shot."

"Where's Beth—" Clint said, looking around and stopping short when he spotted her . . .

DON'T MISS THESE
ALL-ACTION WESTERN SERIES
FROM THE BERKLEY PUBLISHING GROUP

THE GUNSMITH by J. R. Roberts
Clint Adams was a legend among lawmen, outlaws, and ladies. They called him . . . the Gunsmith.

LONGARM by Tabor Evans
The popular long-running series about Deputy U.S. Marshal Custis Long—his life, his loves, his fight for justice.

SLOCUM by Jake Logan
Today's longest-running action Western. John Slocum rides a deadly trail of hot blood and cold steel.

BUSHWHACKERS by B. J. Lanagan
An action-packed series by the creators of Longarm! The rousing adventures of the most brutal gang of cutthroats ever assembled—Quantrill's Raiders.

DIAMONDBACK by Guy Brewer
Dex Yancey is Diamondback, a Southern gentleman turned con man when his brother cheats him out of the family fortune. Ladies love him. Gamblers hate him. But nobody pulls one over on Dex . . .

WILDGUN by Jack Hanson
The blazing adventures of mountain man Will Barlow—from the creators of Longarm!

TEXAS TRACKER by Tom Calhoun
J. T. Law: the most relentless—and dangerous—manhunter in all Texas. Where sheriffs and posses fail, he's the best man to bring in the most vicious outlaws—for a price.

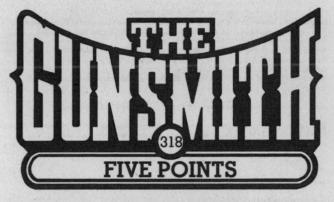

THE GUNSMITH

318

FIVE POINTS

J. R. ROBERTS

JOVE BOOKS, NEW YORK

THE BERKLEY PUBLISHING GROUP
Published by the Penguin Group
Penguin Group (USA) Inc.
375 Hudson Street, New York, New York 10014, USA
Penguin Group (Canada), 90 Eglinton Avenue East, Suite 700, Toronto, Ontario M4P 2Y3, Canada
(a division of Pearson Penguin Canada Inc.)
Penguin Books Ltd., 80 Strand, London WC2R 0RL, England
Penguin Group Ireland, 25 St. Stephen's Green, Dublin 2, Ireland (a division of Penguin Books Ltd.)
Penguin Group (Australia), 250 Camberwell Road, Camberwell, Victoria 3124, Australia
(a division of Pearson Australia Group Pty. Ltd.)
Penguin Books India Pvt. Ltd., 11 Community Centre, Panchsheel Park, New Delhi—110 017, India
Penguin Group (NZ), 67 Apollo Drive, Rosedale, North Shore 0632, New Zealand
(a division of Pearson New Zealand Ltd.)
Penguin Books (South Africa) (Pty.) Ltd., 24 Sturdee Avenue, Rosebank, Johannesburg 2196,
South Africa

Penguin Books Ltd., Registered Offices: 80 Strand, London WC2R 0RL, England

This is a work of fiction. Names, characters, places, and incidents either are the product of the author's imagination or are used fictitiously, and any resemblance to actual persons, living or dead, business establishments, events, or locales is entirely coincidental.

FIVE POINTS

A Jove Book / published by arrangement with the author

PRINTING HISTORY
Jove edition / June 2008

Copyright © 2008 by Robert J. Randisi.
Cover illustration by Sergio Giovine.

ISBN: 978-0-515-14473-4

JOVE®
Jove Books are published by The Berkley Publishing Group,
a division of Penguin Group (USA) Inc.,
375 Hudson Street, New York, New York 10014.
JOVE is a registered trademark of Penguin Group (USA) Inc.
The "J" design is a trademark belonging to Penguin Group (USA) Inc.

PRINTED IN THE UNITED STATES OF AMERICA

10 9 8 7 6 5 4 3 2 1

ONE

Clint Adams sat back in his chair and stared across the table at his friend Talbot Roper. Roper was an ex-Pinkerton who had gone out on his own ten years ago and had made a name for himself as possibly the best private detective in the country—perhaps the world. But they were about to get into a debate on that subject.

Also seated at the table was a mutual friend, Bat Masterson. They had all just finished a sumptuous meal in the dining room of the Denver House Hotel, where Clint was staying, and were now waiting for their coffee and desserts to be served.

"How long are you staying this time?" Roper asked Clint, who had just arrived in Denver the day before.

"I don't know," Clint said. "I just thought it was time to soak up some Denver culture."

"That means he's lookin' for a poker gamer," Bat Masterson said with a laugh.

"I'm shocked to find you in town," Clint said to Roper. "Usually you're out on some big case."

"At the moment I'm out of big cases," Roper said.

"Maybe the best detective in the country has solved them all?" Clint asked.

"I don't know about the best detective in the country," Roper said.

"You sayin' you're not the best?" Masterson asked. "Humility from the great detective?"

"No," Roper said. "I'm just saying that maybe I'm the best private detective in the country, but not the best detective."

"What other kind is there?" Bat asked.

Roper took the time to light up a cigar before he answered. He offered his two friends one, but they demurred.

"There's a friend of mine in New York by the name of Thomas Byrnes. He's a police detective, and it seems he's making quite a name for himself whipping the New York City Police Department into shape."

"Ah," Bat said. "So you're sayin' he's a better organizer than you are."

"That's for sure," Roper said. "But he's a pretty damned good detective as well."

"And what about your old friend Mr. Pinkerton?" Bat asked.

Clint rolled his eyes and said, "Don't get him started on ol' Allan."

"Me?" Roper asked. "You're the one he doesn't like."

"You're the one who worked for him, learned everything you could, and then went out on your own. He's hated you ever since."

"Hates me because I left his agency and took some big clients with me," Roper pointed out. "What's your excuse?"

"Maybe," Clint said, as the waiter arrived with the coffee and pie, "because I would never work for him in the first place."

"Smart man," Bat said. "That sonofabitch wouldn't know how to tell the truth if his life depended on it."

"Probably because of all the lying he had to do during the war," Roper said.

"Oh yeah," Bat said, "the war's a good reason for everythin', isn't it?"

"How did we get on this subject?" Clint asked, cutting into his peach pie. "I thought we were talking about the best detectives in the country?"

"I still say it's our friend here," Bat said. "Although, if you had worked for Pinkerton and got yourself some trainin', Clint, I'd put my money on you."

"Not me—"

"Bat has a point," Roper said. "You have all the instincts, Clint, and we've worked together often enough for me to know that you'd make a hell of a detective."

"Same with poker," Bat said. "If you devoted all your time to that, you'd be better at it than Luke Short."

"Better than you, Bat?" Roper asked.

Bat laughed.

"Let's not get carried away."

They all laughed and enjoyed their desserts.

In the lobby of the hotel, Clint asked Roper, "Are you in town for long?"

"I told you," Roper said. "I've got nothin' to do. If you want to go to the theater, just let me know."

"If I wanted to go to the theater, it wouldn't be with you, my friend," Clint said. "It would be with a woman."

"Okay," Roper said. "If you want a woman, let me know."

"I think I can get my own women, Tal," Clint said, "but thanks."

"Bat," Roper said, "you going to be in town gambling? Or writing?"

"Maybe neither, maybe both," Bat said. "I haven't decided."

"Well, let me know if you fellas want to have dinner again," Roper said. "Good night, and good luck with the cards."

"He doesn't gamble, does he?" Bat asked Clint.

"Not a lick," Clint said. "It never interested him."

"Too bad," Bat said. "He would've been good at it."

"You know, Bat," Clint said. "He's good at what he's good at, you're good at what you're good at, and—"

"I get the picture, Clint," Bat said. "We should all just keep doin' what we're good at."

"Right."

"Do you want to go and find a poker game?"

"No," Clint said. "I think I'll take a walk and maybe have a drink."

"I've got a game if you want one," Bat said. "Some fellas over at *George's Weekly* are playin'."

"Newspapermen?" Clint asked. "They should keep doing what they're good at. You going to fleece them?"

"What a terrible word," Bat said. "I'm gonna *school* them."

TWO

When Clint came downstairs the next morning, the desk clerk called him over.

"This came for you, sir," the man said, handing Clint an envelope.

"Who brought it?"

"A runner, sir," the man said. "Just a dirty street urchin."

Must have been from Roper, he thought. The detective often used street kids to run errands.

"Thank you."

He walked away from the desk, opened the envelope, and fished out the contents. He was looking at two tickets to a show at the Palace Variety Theater. And there was a handwritten note: *Find yourself a girl and have some fun. Tal.*

Clint smiled and put the tickets in his pocket. They were for the next evening. He'd find a woman to take with him by then.

He left the hotel to go in search of breakfast, which he preferred this morning to eat someplace other than the hotel dining room.

• • •

"See? I told you. It's him."

Bethany excitedly squeezed Ben's arm.

"All right, so it's him," Ben said. "What about it?"

"Do you know what a touch he'd be? How excit-ing?"

"Forget it," Ben said. "You'd be lookin' for trouble. Besides, we got work to do."

"*You* have work to do," she said, poking him in the chest. "My work doesn't even start until yours ends, remember? You better get going."

He pointed his finger at her.

"Beth, don't get into trouble, hear? Ma wouldn't like it."

"You're afraid of your ma, Ben," Bethany reminded him, "but I'm not." She laughed.

"Bethany—"

"Oh, go," she said, pushing him. "Go to work. Don't worry about me. I'll amuse myself."

"That's what I'm afraid of."

Ben left the hotel. When he got to the street, he turned right. Bethany went out after him, spotted his retreating back, then turned left and hurried along, hoping to catch up to Clint Adams.

When Ben reached Mrs. Wellington's house, he knocked on the door. When she opened it, she smiled. She wasn't a bad-looking woman and when she smiled, she looked younger than her fifty-odd years.

"Ben, you came."

"I said I would, Libby," he replied.

"Come in, my beautiful boy, come in," she said.

He followed her in and closed the door behind him.

As usual the house was stuffy—but filled with so many valuable things.

"I wasn't sure you'd come," she said, "not after last time."

"I'm sorry," he said. "Last time I was . . . rude."

"No, no," she said. "It's all right. I was . . . foolish. Would you like some tea?"

"I would love some tea, Libby."

"Excellent," she said. "Excellent. We'll have some tea and talk."

"Yes," he said, "we'll talk."

Bethany caught up to Clint Adams as he was going into a small restaurant. She waited. When she was sure he was seated, she went and looked in the window. He was alone, ordering breakfast.

She caught her reflection in the window. She was nineteen and pretty, but not beautiful. Clint Adams only liked beautiful women—at least that was what she'd heard.

She knew she had a few days to play with. Ben wasn't going to be able to get what they wanted from Mrs. Wellington until he gave her what she wanted. He hadn't been ready to do it last time, but he was supposed to be ready now.

Maybe.

She had time, though. Time to watch Clint Adams, time to wait for her chance. If she could successfully pick the Gunsmith's pocket, she would make a name for herself back home in New York. Even Ben's mother would have to admit that. That old witch would have to give her some respect, then.

She'd have to.

THREE

The next night Clint took a woman named Laura Bedford to the theater with him. He had met her the previous night in the hotel bar. They'd had a drink together, then another, and then he'd told her he had two tickets to the theater, and if she was still going to be in town he'd like to take her. She'd agreed.

She met him in the lobby, breathtaking in a red gown. She wore a shawl around her shoulders, and it covered her well, but hinted of dark cleavage beneath. She was tall, made even taller by the fact that she had piled her chestnut hair atop her head.

The show was a lively musical that ended with a big production number that sent everyone away with their toes still tapping.

"A late dinner?" he asked Laura.

"Yes, I'm famished."

Clint had asked Bat Masterson to recommend a restaurant he could take Laura Bedford to. Bat had suggested a place called Brentwood's Steak House. As it turned out, it was a good choice.

"This is marvelous," Laura said, taking a second bite of her steak. "How did you find this place?"

"It was recommended to me by a friend."

"The same friend who gave you the tickets?"

"No," he said, "that was a different friend."

"You have a lot of friends in Denver?"

"A few," he said. "I come here from time to time."

"To get away from the old West?" she asked.

He looked at her, surprised.

"Yes, I recognized your name when you introduced yourself last night," she said. "I know who you are."

"Oh."

"Oh, don't worry," she said. "I would have accepted your invitation even if you weren't the infamous Gunsmith. You're very charming."

"Thank you."

"How long are you planning to stay in Denver?"

"I'm not sure," he said. "As you said, I'm taking a break from the old West. Although, I think the old West is sort of getting away from us. Don't you think?"

"Progress, Mr. Adams," she said. "There's really no way to stop it, is there?"

"No, Miss Bedford," he said, "there isn't."

After dinner they grabbed a hansom cab back to the Denver House, where they went to the bar for a nightcap. Clint had a beer, and Laura Bedford had a snifter of brandy.

"Well, I have to thank you for a lovely evening," she said while they sat and had their drinks.

"Well, it's not quite over yet, is it?" Clint asked.

"No," she said, "not quite." She swirled the brandy

that was left in her glass. "This is a little early for a man like you to be calling it a night, isn't it?" she asked.

"A man like me?"

"Someone who leads as exciting a life as you do," she said. "Don't you have to go and meet some friends for a poker game, or some kind of gambling? Maybe get into a fight or two?"

"My fighting days have moved along with progress, I'm afraid," he said. "And no, I don't have a poker game tonight."

"So that means you're free?" she asked. "Um, like for the whole . . . night?"

"I'm definitely free," he said, "for anyone who has an idea how to spend the whole night."

"Well, if you're not put off by forward-thinking women," she said, "I definitely have an idea . . ."

FOUR

They debated briefly about whose room to go back to, and then they chose hers simply because it was the closest to the lobby.

When they were in her room, she released the shawl and let it fall to the floor. She'd kept it around her the entire night, tantalizing him with an occasional peek at her shadowy cleavage. Now he could see the slopes of her full breasts clearly, but he wanted to see more. He went to her and slid the gown off her shoulders so that it fell first to her waist and then to the floor. She had some wispy underthings on, and once he got rid of those, she was standing in front of him naked and confident. She smiled, pushed her chest against him, and kissed him slowly, deeply. He slid his hands down her back so he could cup her buttocks and pull her closer. She moaned into his mouth and writhed against him, then backed away from him so she could undress him. When she found the little New Line Colt he used as a hideaway gun, he took it from her and placed it on the table next to the bed.

"Can't be too careful, huh?" she asked.

"Never," he said.

She continued to undress him, helped him with his boots and his pants, and then they fell onto her bed together. She was tall and slender, yet full-breasted. He took her in his arms, kissed her lips, her neck, her breasts, all the while stroking her between her legs with his fingertips, causing her to catch her breath.

"God," she said, "your touch is so light."

"We're just getting started," he told her. "I get rougher as we go on."

She laughed deep in her throat and said, "Promise?"

He continued to stroke her until she was very wet, and then kissed his way down her body, saying, "I want to taste you."

"Taste me?" she asked, putting her hands on his head. "I want you to devour me."

When he touched his tongue to her, she jumped as if she'd been struck by lightning, then she sighed and relaxed as his lips and tongue went to work.

"Oh, you're very, very good at this," she whispered.

This time he laughed and said, "I know. You're so sweet, though, I don't want to waste time talking . . ." and went back to work. He licked and sucked her, kissed her, stroked her, pushed his fingers inside of her, inciting her to become more and more excited. Finally, when she could hardly stand it anymore, he moved up over her and slowly entered her until the length of him was enveloped in her warmth.

"Ah, yes," she said as he began to move in and out. "Yes, yes, this is what I was thinking about during that show."

"Really?" he said against her ear. "You mean we wasted all that time watching that terrible show?"

They both laughed.

"Well," she said, wrapping her legs around his waist, "we're not wasting any more, are we?"

She pulled his head down and thrust her tongue deeply into his mouth . . .

They lay together later, regaining their breath, her head on his shoulders, their naked bodies still pressed together.

"You were right," he said. "That was a good idea."

"And the night's not over yet," she told him.

"No," he said, "not by a long shot."

When Ben opened the door to their hotel room and entered, he shouted, "Bethany!"

"I'm here," she said from the bed. She was fully dressed and had been reading a book. "How did it go?"

"It was no fun, believe me," he said, taking off his jacket and throwing it down.

"Oh, come on," Bethany said. "She's not that bad-lookin'."

"She's old," Ben said. "Her skin was . . . like leather."

She put her arms around him from behind and hugged.

"There, there," she said. "My brave boy."

"I'm not a boy," he said. "I'm twenty-two."

"I know," she said. "Are we all set for tomorrow?"

He put his hand in his pocket and came out with the

key to Mrs. Wellington's house. Bethany snatched it from his hand.

"Finally!"

"You try sleepin' with some fifty-year-old man and see how fast you get it done," he said.

"I'm proud of you, Ben," she said, "and your mama is gonna be proud, too."

FIVE

The next morning Clint woke, got out of bed without waking Laura, and went back to his own room. He slept another two hours there, then had a bath and dressed for the day. There had been nothing said about meeting the next day, so he decided to leave it to chance. Besides, this was the day he had put aside to find a poker game. He was to meet Bat for lunch at one of his favorite restaurants, Del Frisco's.

Because he knew his lunch with Bat would be sumptuous, he decided to have a light breakfast, just coffee and biscuits, so he went right into the Denver House's dining room. He ordered food, the *Denver Post*, and the newspaper that Bat had mentioned, *George's Weekly*.

He spent some leisure time getting refills on the coffee and reading through both newspapers. Roper, notorious for being in the papers, was not mentioned in either. Neither was Bat. Clint figured his two friends had been keeping their heads down lately and staying out of trouble.

Which, of course, wasn't their way. Sooner or later

they'd find trouble—or trouble would find them—just
as it would happen to him. There was no way any of
them could avoid it.

But he couldn't get into trouble just sitting here
reading the newspapers, could he?

Ben and Bethany met Willie O'Donnell on the corner
near their hotel, down the street from the Denver
House. Ben's mother had given them enough money to
stay in style.

"Got it?" O'Donnell asked.

Bethany held the key out to him.

"Thanks, little darlin'," he said, giving her an ugly
smile. "I guess that means our boy Ben did his dirty
job, huh?"

Bethany squeezed Ben's arm to keep him from
protesting. Willie O'Donnell called him a boy to get
his goat. She only did it to tease him. He didn't like it,
either way, but if he spoke up, Willie would give him a
beating.

"You got your men ready?" Bethany asked.

"Aye," O'Donnell said. "We're ready to go. What
about our Ben here?"

"Ben will do his part, Willie," Bethany said. "He'll
get the woman out of the house for hours."

"Good, good," Willie said.

"Noon, Willie," Bethany said. "Don't forget."

"Aye, lass," Willie said. "Noon. You wouldn't want
to get together with me before then, would ye?"

"Good-bye, Willie," Bethany said. "See you in New
York."

Willie grinned at them, showing gaps where teeth
used to be. Each of the missing teeth had been

knocked out in some fight or another, some on the streets of New York, others in places like Sing Sing Prison.

"I hate him," Ben said as Willie walked away.

"Yeah, but your mama doesn't."

"I don't know why she puts up with him."

"Don't you?"

Ben winced. "I don't want to hear that, Bethany."

"You have one last job to do today, Ben," Bethany said. "Then we're on the train back home."

"I can't wait to get home," Ben said. "We've been away too long."

"You always wanted to see the West, Ben."

"The old West, Beth," he said. "Denver is just like New York."

"You mean the old West of Wild Bill Hickok, Billy the Kid, and the Gunsmith?"

"Billy the Kid was from New York," Ben said, "and I told you to stay away from Clint Adams."

"I haven't gone anywhere near him," she said, showing Ben her open hands. "I swear."

"Keep it that way," Ben said. "We're almost done here, we don't need trouble from some relic of the old West."

"He doesn't look like much of a relic," she said.

He shook his head.

"I hate to leave you alone, Bethany," he said. "You're gonna get yourself in trouble."

"I'll be fine, Ben," she said. "I am not gonna get myself in trouble."

"When did you stop saying 'ain't'?" he asked.

"I haven't said ain't for a long time, Ben. I've left a lot of the street behind me."

"I didn't notice."

"I know."

Ben started away, then stopped.

"You can't leave Five Points too far behind you, Bethany," he said. "It just can't be done."

She smiled.

"You mean it just ain't done, don't you, Ben?"

SIX

At lunch, Bat said, "So, you were out with a real lady last night."

"You certainly weren't at the theater," Clint said. "You couldn't have gone unnoticed."

"No, I wasn't there."

"Then how do you know who I was with?"

"I have eyes and ears," Bat said, "all over town."

"Why would you need to have Denver that well covered?" Clint asked.

"I'm thinkin' about puttin' down roots here," Bat said. "Emma likes it."

"Do *you* like it?"

"I like it fine."

"Not going to happen, Bat."

"Why not?"

"Because you can't put down roots," Clint said. "It just isn't in you."

"What makes you think you know me so damned well?" Bat demanded.

Clint smiled. "Years of experience."

Bat maintained a sullen silence for a good five

minutes, then said, "There are plenty of poker games here."

"You need a challenge."

"I could do very well here," Bat said. "I could start writin'."

"Writing?"

"For *George's Weekly*," Bat said. "They want me to do a sports column."

"What do you know about writing?"

"How hard could it be?" Bat asked. "You dip a pen in some ink, you start writin'. Have you read the newspapers here? There's a bunch of idiots writin' columns."

"So you think you'd fit right in?"

"Ha-ha," Bat said. "I'd be head and shoulders above a lot of 'em."

"Well," Clint said, "if that's what you want to do, I'm all for it. Go to it. Enjoy it."

"Thank you."

"While it lasts."

"You gotta have the last word, don't you?"

Clint put his knife and fork down, looked across the table at his friend, and said, "Yes."

Bat gave Clint the location of a likely poker game as they left the restaurant.

"Not your newspaper cronies?" Clint asked.

"No," Bat said, "gamblers. Bankers, publishers, politicians—and you."

"Not you?"

"Not tonight," Bat said, "but you've been introduced. Just asked for Bill Finch."

"Bill Finch."

Bat nodded.

"He'll let you in. You got the location?"

"I've got it. What are you up to tonight?"

"There's a prizefight I'm gonna attend," Bat said, "and then I'm gonna try writin' about it."

"Who's fighting?"

"Nobody," Bat said. "This is just for practice. You've got a lot of time before the game. What're you gonna be doin'?"

"Well, after that meal—thank you very much, by the way—I think I'll take a walk."

"You're heeled, I take it," Bat said, "so that should be okay."

Clint took the New Line out from behind his back, showed it to Bat, and put it back.

"Should get yourself a shoulder rig if you're gonna stay around long," Bat said. "It'd fit under that jacket just fine."

"I've been using this New Line as a holdout gun for a long time," Clint said. "It'll do."

"Suit yourself," Bat said. "You always do. I'll check in with you at your hotel tomorrow to see how you did."

"Come by for breakfast."

"Not gonna be havin' breakfast with your new conquest?" Bat asked.

"Don't know how that's going," Clint said, "but even if she's there, I'm sure she'd love to meet you. She seems to think the old West has passed us all by."

"Guess she's not far wrong," Bat said. "Sounds like a smart gal."

"Smart's the least of her appeal."

"Knowin' you, I expect her to be a beauty. Okay, breakfast it is."

The two friends shook hands and went their separate ways.

SEVEN

Later that night Willie O'Donnell met with Ben and Bethany in their hotel room.

"I can't believe you did that," Bethany said to Willie. "Are you stupid?"

"Careful, little girl," Willie said.

"Don't threaten her," Ben said.

Willie turned his murderous gaze on Ben. Bethany was not afraid of Willie for herself, but she knew the crazy Irishman would kill Ben in the wink of an eye.

"Never mind," Bethany said. "We have to get out of Denver tomorrow."

"I'm still sticking to the plan," Willie said. "My boys and I are leavin' tomorrow."

"Good," Bethany said. "Ben and I will be on a train in the morning."

"So it's over," Willie said. "We did it."

"It ain't over," Ben said. "Ma's gonna be mad at you, Willie."

"I ain't afraid of your ma, little man," Willie said. "And it ain't my fault you came back too early and let her go in the house."

Bethany stared at Willie and wondered, if Ben had gone into the house with Libby Wellington, would Willie have killed him, too?

"With the woman dead the police are gonna be lookin' for a killer, not just a swindler," Bethany said. "I think Ma is gonna be mad at all of us."

"Maybe," Willie said, "until I get there with the merchandise." Willie pointed a finger at Ben. "You and Bethany will get to New York before I do. Don't be bad-mouthin' me to your old lady, ya hear?"

"I'm just gonna tell her what happened," Ben said, "that's all."

"That better be all, boyo," Willie said.

"That's enough," Bethany said. "Get out now, Willie. We'll see you in New York."

"I'm goin'," Willie said, but he pointed at Ben one last time. "Remember, boyo."

Willie left.

"I told you he's crazy," Ben said. "He didn't have to kill Libby."

"It's done, Ben," Bethany said. "It's over. We have to leave. We'll go to the station and get on the first train."

He sat down on the bed with his hands clasped between his knees. For a moment she thought he was going to fall forward.

She sat next to him, put her arm around his shoulders.

"It's not your fault."

"She wanted to come back early," he said. "I tried to talk her out of it, but I couldn't." He shook his head. "I should've gone in with her."

"I'm afraid if you had, Willie might have killed you, too."

"You're probably right."

"I'll tell your mama is wasn't your fault."

"It ain't that," he said. "She was a nice lady, that's all. She didn't deserve to die."

"I know," Bethany said. "I know."

He put his head on her shoulder and she held him that way. Later, she put him in his bed, hoping he'd fall asleep.

She went to the window and looked out. They had to flee Denver now, and she'd never get a chance at the Gunsmith. She blamed Willie and his stupidity for that.

Tal Roper got out of the carriage and stopped in front of the house. Captain Leo Delaney came walking over to him.

"Sorry, Tal," he said. "I knew she was a client of yours, that's why I sent word."

"She was a client, yes," Roper said. She'd hired him months ago to find some of her relatives, but he had come up empty. Apparently, Libby Wellington was alone in the world.

"What happened?" he asked.

"Seems she came home and surprised a burglar," Delaney said. "Bashed her head in with a lamp."

"Burglar?"

"Well, thieves, anyway."

"What do you mean?"

"Looks like they got in with a key and were cleaning out the place. Did she have a lot of expensive things?"

"Yes," Roper said. "That's about all she had. Paintings, furniture, silverware—everything she had was valuable."

"Well then, that explains why everything is gone."

"Everything?"

"A lot of it," Delaney said. "The walls are bare, with markings where frames used to hang. Sofa's gone, some lamps, silverware . . . The whole house looks looted."

"And with a key?" Roper asked. "The door wasn't jimmied? Or the lock picked?"

Delaney shook his head.

"Opened with a key. Whoever did it was slick, figured out a way to get a key."

"Talk to the neighbors?"

"Yeah, looks like she was getting visits from a man—a young man."

"Ah, Jesus," Roper said. "She was lonely, Leo. Some young buck probably conned her."

"It happens."

"You got a description of this young fella?"

"Thought you'd ask," Delaney said. He handed Roper a slip of paper.

"This kind of job," Roper said, "they're going to need a fence for the merchandise."

"Nobody in this town will touch it."

"No," Roper said, "this kind of job would need a fence from somewhere like . . . oh, New York, maybe."

"Funny you should mention that."

"Why?"

"One neighbor said she heard the young fella talkin' to Mrs. Wellington one day. She said he sounded like he was from New York."

"How would she know that?"

"Said she took a trip there last year. Said she'd never forget that accent."

"New York."

"So you headin' for New York?" Delaney asked.

"I just took a big case today," Roper said. "If this was yesterday, I'd be on the first train."

"You feel like you owed this lady something?"

"No, nothing like that," Roper said. "I'd just like to help is all."

"Farm the other case out."

"Can't," Roper said.

"What is it?"

"Can't talk about it."

"Oh," Delaney said, "one of your top-secret government things, huh?"

Roper didn't respond.

"Okay, so farm this one out, then," Delaney said. "How hard can it be to track this stuff? They'll need wagons to get it to New York. Might switch to a train along the way, ship the stuff."

"No," Roper said. "I'd go to New York and wait for them."

"So, get somebody to go for you," Delaney said.

"Captain?" somebody called.

"I gotta go to work, Tal," Delaney said. "I just wanted you to know about this."

"Thanks, Leo."

"I hope you get somebody to help you with this."

"I think," Roper said, "I have just the man."

EIGHT

Clint had done very well at Bat's poker game. The politicians and bankers had been only too glad to give him their money. They were rich men who played bad poker. Those were Clint's favorite kind of wealthy men.

As he entered the hotel lobby, he immediately saw Talbot Roper sitting on one of the lobby sofas.

"Looking for a drink?" Clint asked. "Or a drinking companion?"

"I could use both."

"Come on."

They went into the bar. Clint bought two beers and they went to a table, sitting among the guests and few businessmen who had not yet gone home to their wives.

"What's on your mind?" Clint asked.

Roper told Clint about meeting Libby Wellington, and trying to help her.

"Couldn't find a soul," he finished. "I had to tell her she was all alone in the world."

"Husband?"

"Died ten years ago," Roper said. "Left her fixed well, real well."

"So what's the problem?" Clint asked. "She wants you to look again?"

"She's dead," Roper said. "Somebody killed her tonight."

"How?"

"Bashed her over the head when she walked in on them robbing her house. Then they cleaned her out."

"How bad?"

"Just about everything," Roper said. "Furniture, silverware, whatever they could carry."

"That's a lot of merchandise," Clint said. "What are they going to do with it?"

"Fence it."

"Where do you figure?"

"New York."

"That's a long way to come for some merchandise," Clint said. "Long way to go to fence it."

"It'll fetch a lot, make it worth it."

"So? You going?"

"Can't," Roper said. "I'd like to, but I can't."

"Why not?"

"Took a job earlier today," Roper said. "I have to leave tomorrow."

"Heading?"

"West."

Clint studied his friend for a few minutes, then said, "Oh."

"When's the last time you were in New York?"

"Couple of years, I guess," Clint said, "maybe a little less."

"Maybe it's time for another visit."

"You'll have to tell me what I'm looking for."

"You'll do it?"

"Sure."

"I don't have to try to convince you?"

"You did already."

"How?"

"You asked."

Roper sat back.

"I appreciate it, Clint."

"What are friends for?"

Roper spent the next hour telling Clint what to look for, and how.

"I'll send a telegram tomorrow," he said when he was done. "It'll introduce you to Tom Byrnes."

"Ah, your police detective friend," Clint said. "I've never run across him in New York. He might not be happy to see me."

"Don't worry," Roper said. "He'll talk to you."

"May not like me."

"But he'll talk to you."

They sat and talked for another hour and then walked out to the lobby together.

"Where will you be?" Clint asked. "If I want to get ahold of you."

"Send a telegram to general delivery in San Francisco," Roper said. "It'll get to me."

"All right."

They shook hands.

"Thanks again, Clint."

"Good luck with your job. We'll talk soon."

Roper nodded and left the hotel. Clint turned and went to the desk.

"Is Miss Bedford in her room?"

"Miss Bedford checked out, sir," the clerk said.

"When?"

"This morning."

Clint nodded.

"Thanks."

One night. That was as much as he had expected. He decided to turn in. He had to catch a train to New York tomorrow.

NINE

Clint met Bat Masterson in the dining room for breakfast in the morning.

"Where's your lady?"

"Checked out."

"Too bad."

Clint sat opposite his friend and poured himself some coffee from the pot already on the table.

"How'd you do last night?"

"It was worth the effort."

"Good. They're playin' again tonight. Maybe I'll even join you."

"Not tonight," Clint said. "Not tomorrow night. I'm leaving today."

"That's kind of sudden."

"Something came up kind of sudden."

"Must've been somethin' important."

The waiter came over and they both ordered steak and eggs. As they ate, Clint told Bat about Tal Roper's request.

"That's too bad about the lady," Bat said, "but why is it your business?"

"Roper needed help," Clint said. "He took a job he can't get out of."

"So you're going to New York?"

"Right."

"I kind of like New York," Bat said, "but I'm a little tied up here."

"I wasn't asking."

"Just in case."

"All I have to do is find the killer," Clint said. "I can do that alone."

"What about the merchandise?"

"Roper doesn't care about that," Clint said. "Just the killer."

"So," Bat said, "you're gonna play detective."

"I had a quick lesson last night," Clint said. "So I guess I'm going to do a little more than play at it. Plus, he's sending a telegram to his friend Byrnes."

"Ah," Bat said, "the great police detective. So you won't be so alone, after all."

"I guess not."

Bethany walked over to Ben and handed him his ticket. The train station was empty that early in the morning, not any people leaving Denver.

"Did you send Ma a telegram?" he asked.

"I decided not to," she said. "We'll just tell her when we get there."

"She's gonna be really mad," Ben said.

"Yeah," Bethany said. "At Willie. Come on, let's wait on the platform."

Bethany had been wearing pants and men's shirts the whole time in Denver, but today she had on her traveling dress.

"You look real pretty today," he told her.

She smiled. "That's a nice thing for a brother to say to a sister."

"Half sister," he reminded her.

"You don't have to remind me of that," she said.

"I guess that's why you're not afraid of Mama," he said. "She's not your mother."

"Maybe not," Bethany said, "but she's pretty scary anyway."

"Not to you," Ben said. "You're not afraid of anybody. Not Ma, not Willie . . . not the Gunsmith. Tell me, did you ever pick his pocket?"

"I never got the chance," she said.

"Maybe you will someday."

"No," she said. "I'll probably never get another chance."

As Clint entered the station, a train pulled out. He knew he wouldn't get the first train of the day. Now he had to hope there was another.

"This afternoon, at three," the station clerk told him. "To Chicago."

"Where was that one going?" Clint asked.

"To Saint Louis."

"Okay," Clint said. "I'll take one ticket to Chicago."

"One way?"

"Sure," Clint said, "one way."

Clint paid and collected the ticket. He had plenty of time to make arrangements for Eclipse, his Darley Arabian, to be cared for. Bat had told him what stable to put him up at, and promised to look in on him.

It had been on a trip to New York that P. T. Barnum had made Clint a gift of the stallion.

And last time in New York he'd made the acquaintance of Annie Oakley and had seen Buffalo Bill.

This time he was looking for a killer, and would meet the man Roper felt was the greatest living detective—police detective.

Captain Thomas J. Byrnes.

TEN

George Appo entered his apartment on Mott Street, closed the door, and locked it behind him. He poured himself a drink, then sat down at the table and emptied his pockets. When he'd left that morning, his pockets had been empty. Now what he emptied from them had once been in the pockets of others. Appo was a pickpocket. It was how he made his living. Sometimes pickings were good, and sometimes they weren't. Today they had been good. He spread his booty out on the table. Coins, paper money in wallets, watches. As long as men carried their valuables in their coat pockets or their vest pockets, and as long as women swung their purses or hid them beneath heavy skirts, pickpockets would be able to make a living.

Fredericka Mandelbaum closed her shop and locked the doors. She went into the office in the back of the shop where she kept her ledgers. The dry goods store was a losing proposition. She had one ledger that showed that clearly. But from her desk she took another ledger. This was the one she made her living with. Not only was she the only female fence in town, but she was also one of the most successful fences of all. She was known to many, but by different names. "Old Woman," "Mother Baum," or just plain "Mother." But the one she liked the best was "Queen of Fences." She didn't know who had named her that, but she liked it.

She looked at the calendar on her wall. Ben and Bethany should be back in a few days. Willie and his men a few days after that. Once they had returned from their trip out West, there would be plenty more to put in the ledger.

Plenty.

Captain Thomas J. Byrnes sat at his desk on Mulberry Street and reread the telegram from his friend Talbot Roper. Talbot was sending his friend Clint Adams to New York, and wanted Byrnes to give him as much help as possible. Help with what, the telegram didn't say. But Byrnes knew who the Gunsmith was, and he knew Roper wouldn't ask for help unless it was something important.

Byrnes, who had started out as a fireman in Manhattan, had worked his way up to chief of detectives. It was by his hand that the New York City Police Department had become one of the greatest in the country—in the world. Manhattan was a city where there was no place for men like Clint Adams. The gunmen of the West needed to stay in the West and die there with it.

But Adams was coming here, and Byrnes owed it to Roper to help him.

He checked his watch, stood up, put on his gun and jacket, and left for the station.

When the knock came at the door, Fredericka Mandelbaum frowned. Who'd be banging on her door now? It was time for her lunch.

She walked to the door and opened it. When she saw Bethany and Ben standing there, she said, "Aw, hell."

"Hello, Ma—" Ben said, but she cut him off with a slap to the face.

"The only reason you'd be back early is if somethin' went wrong," she said.

"It wasn't his fault, Ma," Bethany said.

"You're always tryin' to stick up for him," Fredericka said. "Come in here, both of you."

She grabbed Ben by the front of the shirt and pulled him inside. Bethany followed.

"Where's Willie?" Ma asked.

"He's comin' with the merchandise," Ben said.

"So you got the merchandise?" his mother asked.

"Yeah."

"Then what's the problem?" she demanded. "Come on, why'd you come runnin' back home so soon?"

"It was Willie," Bethany said. "He killed the Wellington woman."

"Killed her? Why?"

"She came home early, while he and his boys were still there."

Fredericka narrowed her eyes at her stepdaughter, whom she had never liked.

"You're always tryin' to blame Willie for everything," she said.

"That's because he *is* to blame for everything," Bethany said. "Willie's an idiot."

Fredericka swung her hand at Bethany, who ducked away. She would not stand for being hit the way Ben did.

"Whose job was it to keep the woman away?" the older woman demanded.

"It was mine," Ben said.

She slapped him.

"Willie didn't have to kill the woman!" Bethany shouted. "Now the Denver police are looking for a murderer."

"Well, they ain't gonna look in New York, are they?" Fredericka asked.

"You're always stickin' up for Willie because he warms your bed," Bethany said.

"You get out of here, girl," Fredericka said. "You're just mad because you twitch your little ass at Willie and he ain't interested. He wants a real woman."

"You mean an *old* woman, don't you?" Bethany asked.

"Get her outta here, Ben," Fredericka said. "I'll talk to Willie when he gets back, find out what really happened, and then we'll all talk again. Now get . . . her . . . outta here!"

"Come on, Ben," Bethany said, grabbing her half brother's arm.

"Bethany did good, Ma," Ben said, "real good."

"Ah," Fredericka said, "you're a sick boy, in love with your own sister!"

Bethany dragged Ben outside.

ELEVEN

Byrnes had two stops to make before he arrived at Grand Central Station to await Clint Adams's arrival. While waiting, he recognized three different pickpockets in the crowd, all children. When they saw him, they all did a disappearing act. Byrnes was known to look upon pickpockets with grave disapproval.

He had done some research on Clint Adams, otherwise known as the Gunsmith. Most of what he'd read he took with a grain of salt. Of course the man had a reputation, but it was surely exaggerated, along with those of Billy the Kid and Jesse James. Surely, no one could live up to such a reputation. It was fodder for the dime novels of Ned Buntline and his ilk. He knew Adams had come to New York from time to time, but their paths had never crossed before.

Of course, since Adams was given Roper's recommendation, the man had to have something to recommend him. Byrnes had agreed to meet him and talk to him, but beyond that he'd form his own opinion of the man, and only then would he decide whether or not to assist him.

He stayed off the train platform, preferring to wait instead inside the terminal building. During his time there very little, if any, pickpocket business was conducted.

When the train pulled into the station, Clint remained seated. The car was crowded, and he saw no reason to push out the doors with the rest of the passengers.

When there was some elbow room to move, he rose and stepped out onto the platform. He could not remember the platform being this crowded on any of his other trips to New York. Obviously, the city had continued to grow in his absence. He knew if he stayed away for another ten years and then returned, he would not recognize the place.

As he moved toward the terminal, he was bumped several times, but the last time he reached down and snatched a small hand from his pocket.

"Sorry, sir," the boy said, smiling up at him.

"Yes, you are."

The boy pulled, but Clint did not let go.

"Can I go now, sir?" the boy said. "I'm sorry. I needed money for my sick mother. I've never done something like this before."

"Yes, you have," Clint said. "Your touch was quite good."

The boy studied him, then smiled genuinely.

"Yes, sir, I do have a good touch," he said. "No one's ever caught me before. You must be very good yourself."

"I'm very good at keeping my property in my pockets," Clint said.

Finally, he released the boy's hand, but the youngster—probably ten or eleven—did not move.

"You've been to New York before, huh?"

"Yes, I have."

"Then you don't need a guide?"

"No."

"I could get you a cab, sir."

"I can get my own cab."

"Then there's nothin' I can do for you?"

"You can keep your hands out of my pockets," Clint said.

The boy grinned, revealing one missing tooth on the bottom.

"My name's Red, sir," he said.

"Your hair's black," Clint pointed out.

"Yes, sir, it's not a nickname, it's my real name," the boy said. "Red. You need anythin' at all while you're in New York, you ask for Red."

"Ask who?"

"Anyone, sir," the boy said. "Everybody on the street knows Red."

"Red, why are you working the platform when there are more pockets than you can shake a stick at out in the terminal?"

"Ah, but the top cop is in the terminal."

"Top cop?"

"Captain Byrnes, sir," Red said. "Chief of detectives. He don't like pickpockets, not at all."

"What does Captain Byrnes look like?"

"Kinda sad lookin', with a big mustache," Red said.

"You won't be able to miss him, sir, because of his uniform."

"Ah . . ." Clint said, but before he could say anything else the boy was gone.

Clint left the platform and entered the terminal. The man in uniform was not hard to find. It was as if he had a fence around him. People were giving him a wide berth.

"How did you know I'd find you?" Clint asked him.

Byrnes smiled. "How could you not, Mr. Adams?"

The two men shook hands.

"Are you wearing a gun?" Byrnes asked.

"Yes."

"I don't see a holster."

"My holster is in my bag," Clint said. "The gun is tucked into my belt, at the small of my back."

"Your Peacemaker?"

"I carry a small New Line Colt in my belt," Clint said. "My regular Colt is in my bag."

"How long have you known Roper?"

"Many years."

"Yes," Byrnes said. "I, too, have known him many years."

"So he said."

"What else did he say about me?" Byrnes asked.

"You only come up when someone calls him the greatest detective in the country."

"What does he say?"

"He says your name."

Byrnes smiled.

"He says he's the greatest private detective in the country, doesn't he?"

"He says he may be the greatest private detective in

the world," Clint said, "but you are the greatest police detective."

Byrnes extended his hand again, and this time they shook more firmly.

"Welcome to New York, Mr. Adams."

TWELVE

Byrnes asked Clint what kind of a hotel he wanted to stay in. Clint told him something small and discreet.

"I don't want to be noticed."

Byrnes had his driver take them to a small hotel near Union Square.

"There's no bar," Byrnes said, "but there's a small tavern next door there." He pointed. "There's never any trouble there."

"Why is that?"

"Because I drink there."

"Why don't we go in and have a drink now?" Clint suggested.

"I'll have my driver check you in, take your bag to your room, and then bring you the key."

"That's fine."

Byrnes made those arrangements, then led the way into the tavern, which had no name above the door. It was warm inside, cozy. The bartender nodded to the captain, who did not seem concerned about being in the tavern while in uniform. Likewise, the patrons did not give him a second look.

"They expect me to come in and out of here," Byrnes said, leading Clint to a table in the back. "Nobody even blinks anymore, unless there's a stranger here, and then he's quickly advised to turn his head away."

A barmaid came over and graced them with a smile and a pair of impressive breasts, which were threatening to leap from her peasant blouse. Her nipples seemed as big as a puppy dog's nose.

"What can I get for you gents?" she asked.

"Two beers, Angie," Byrnes said.

"Comin' up, Captain," she said, but before leaving she asked, "Who's your handsome friend?"

"This is Clint . . ." Byrnes almost said the last name, but caught himself.

"Welcome to the tavern, Clint."

"Angie, the beers?"

"Comin' up, Captain."

She turned and sashayed back to the bar so Clint could watch her round bottom.

"Roper didn't say what he wanted me to help you with," Byrnes said, "just that he wanted me to help you."

"Roper had a client who was killed in Denver," Clint said. "A lady. Seems she walked in on some men looting her home."

"They killed her? How?"

"Hit her over the head with a lamp."

"Why's he not looking into this himself?"

"He had just taken a job he couldn't get out of," Clint said. "He asked me to come in his stead."

"And you agreed?"

"That's what friends are for."

"What makes Roper think the killer came to New York?" Byrnes asked.

"He figures this is the best place for them to fence the goods they stole," Clint said.

"What kind of goods are we talkin' about?" Byrnes asked.

"Furniture, silverware, housewares," Clint said. "They just about cleaned the house out."

Byrnes rubbed his jaw.

"We got quite a few fences in Manhattan who can handle that kind of merchandise," Byrnes said. "I'll put the word out and see what I can find out."

"I don't guess they'd be here yet," Clint said. "They've got to be pulling two, three wagons with them."

"They'll be days behind you, then," Byrnes said. "I can still find out which fence is waitin' for a haul that big."

"I'd be much obliged, Captain."

"Call me Tom," Byrnes said. "Tell me, Mr. Adams—"

"Call me Clint, Tom."

"Okay, Clint," Byrnes said. "Knowing Tal Roper the way I do, he's concerned with the merchandise second."

"You're right," Clint said. "He's more concerned with who killed Mrs. Wellington."

"Seems to me you might have come here a little too quickly, Clint," Byrnes said. "You probably should've snooped around a little more in Denver. Now you've got some days to kill."

Clint sat back in his chair as Angie came back with their beers. She leaned over him and he could smell the sweet fragrance wafting up from between her breasts.

"You boys tell me if you need anything else."

Clint could think of quite a few things, but not right at that moment.

"Thanks, Angie."

As she walked away, he looked at Byrnes.

"Roper was right. You are smart," Clint said. "Guess I should've looked into it a bit in Denver."

"Roper probably would've thought of it himself if he wasn't upset about the woman," Byrnes said.

"You're right," Clint said.

"Is there somebody else in Denver who might look into it for you?" Byrnes asked.

"As a matter of fact, there is," Clint said. "I'll send a telegram as soon as I can."

"Who we talking about?"

"Bat Masterson."

Byrnes raised his eyebrows over his beer mug.

"Sounds like you have some pretty impressive friends, Clint."

"Bat was going to hang around Denver for a while," Clint said. "He should still be there."

"There's a telegraph office right down the street," Byrnes said. "We can finish these beers and I'll take you over there. Then I better get back to work."

"And I'll get settled at the hotel."

"Which hotel?" Angie asked, coming up on them. "Just thought I'd check on you boys, and I overheard you."

"I'm staying next door," Clint said.

"Well," she said, "that'll be pretty handy. I mean, we've got some good food here. Come on over when you get hungry."

"I will," Clint promised.

She smiled and hip-switched away again.

THIRTEEN

Bethany and Ben entered their boardinghouse together. Neither of them lived with Fredericka Mandelbaum. She had put them both out before they were of age. They each had their own room in the boardinghouse, which was owned by a widow in her eighties.

In the hall Bethany asked, "Ben, why do you put up with her?"

"She's my ma, Bethany," he said. "Yours, too."

"She ain't my ma," Bethany said with feeling.

Ben laughed.

"What's so funny?"

"You got your ain't back."

"You and me, Ben," she said. "We've got to go out on our own."

"Bethany—"

"I'm goin' in my room," she said. "Let me know when you want to get something to eat."

"Bethany—" Ben said again, but she went into her room and closed the door behind her.

•   •   •

Clint walked down to the telegraph office with Byrnes, then told the captain he'd be okay on his own.

"That's right," Byrnes said. "You've been to New York a time or two, haven't you?"

"That's right," Clint said. "I know my way around pretty well."

"Well, my office is on Mulberry Street," Byrnes said. "You come and see me if you need anything. Meanwhile, I'll be looking into those fences."

"Thanks, Tom. I appreciate it. I'm sure Tal will, too."

"Let me know if you hear from him, will you?" Byrnes asked.

"I'll let you know."

Byrnes went off to do his job while Clint went into the telegraph office and sent a missive off to Bat Masterson in Denver.

"Where will you be, sir, for a reply?" the clerk asked.

"I'm at the hotel down the street," Clint said. "I'm sorry, I don't know the name of it yet."

"That's the Belvedere," the clerk said. "I'll leave any reply at the desk. I know the clerks there."

"Thanks."

Clint left the office and walked back to his hotel to get settled. Then he realized he hadn't gotten the room key from Captain Byrnes's driver. Well, maybe they'd left it at the front desk for him.

As he was walking past the tavern, the door opened and Angie came running out. Her breasts were bobbing and Clint couldn't take his eyes off them.

"The captain's driver brought your key, Clint, but you were gone, so I kept it for you."

"Thanks a lot, Angie."

She smiled at him, then reached between her breasts and came out with the key.

"Thought I'd keep it there for safekeeping."

She put it in his hand.

"It's warm," he said. "Real warm. Thanks again, Angie."

"You come back real soon, Clint. I'll make sure you get the best meal in the house."

"I'll make a point of it, Angie."

He held the door for her, catching the fragrance of her again as she went inside.

Clint introduced himself to the desk clerk and waved the key to show that he had it.

"The captain's man put your bag in your room, mister," the clerk said. "My name's Owen. If you need anything, you let me know."

"Thanks. I will."

Clint went up to his room, which was on the second of three floors. When he entered, he found it small but neat and clean. His bag was on the bed. He decided to unpack it and make some use of the dresser drawers. Byrnes had been very right. Roper or Clint should have thought to do some investigating in Denver before he hopped on a train. He just hoped too much time hadn't gone by, and maybe Bat would be able to find out something helpful.

When he finished, he poured some water from the pitcher into the basin on top of the dresser. He washed his hands and face and, while drying, realized he was hungry. Or maybe he just wanted to go back to the tavern and talk to Angie some more. Or see what else she kept in her cleavage besides hotel keys.

FOURTEEN

When George Appo spotted the boy Red on the street, he called him over.

"How'd you do today, young man?"

"Not so good, George," Red said. "I went to Grand Central Station, but wouldn't ya know it, the cap'n was there."

"Byrnes? What was he doin' at the train station?" Appo asked.

"Meetin' somebody, I guess," Red said. "I tried pickin' this gent's pocket, but he weren't no sucker."

"He caught you?"

"Slick as you please."

"And let you go?"

"Yup."

"And then what?"

"I watched him," Red said. "He met up with the cap'n, they shook hands, and then the cap'n drove him away."

"To where?"

"Didn't see," Red said. "I thought once the cap'n was gone I'd get some work done, but the terminal was

emptying out and there weren't another train for another couple of hours."

"You should have waited."

"I thought I'd go over to Times Square and do some
business but it was slim pickins."

"Are you hungry?"

"I sure am."

"Well, come on," Appo said. "I'm goin' over to the
Metropole for some supper."

"Metropole?" Red said, shaking his head. "They
ain't gonna let me in there, George."

"They will if you're with me," Appo said.

"You're the best, George."

"That's what they tell me."

And, indeed, Appo—the son of the notorious Quimbo
Appo, thief and murderer—was the best pickpocket in
all of Manhattan. Quimbo was Asian, and Appo's
mother was Irish. Like his father, Appo was not a large
man. He had even been described as diminutive, but
unlike his father, he was a dapper dresser who kept
himself well-appointed. When he wasn't picking pockets, he was running cons. But he had never killed anyone, and so was not "notorious" like his father. Rather,
he was "infamous" among the lowlifes of Manhattan,
who pretty much all looked up to him.

Among those was Bethany, who was a protégé of
Appo. She was waiting on the steps of the Metropole
when Appo arrived with Red in tow. At nineteen she
was less than ten years younger than George, but there
was nothing romantic between them. Rather he saw
her as someone he could pass his experiences on to,

and she had the best set of hands he'd ever seen on a pickpocket, man or woman. She truly had "the touch."

"Where's Ben?" Appo asked.

"Oh, he's sulkin' in his room," Bethany said.

"About what?"

"I'll tell you over supper. Hello, Red."

"Miss Bethany."

Red blushed furiously every time Bethany spoke to him, because his ten-year-old heart belonged to her. She ruffled his hair and said, "You could use a face washin'."

"Aw, Miss Bethany . . ."

"Well, work on him at our table," Appo said. "A napkin and a glass of water and we'll spruce the boy up. Come on, I'm starved. You have to tell me and Red all about your trip out West."

"Did you see any Indians, Miss Bethany?" Red asked.

"No," Bethany said, "but I saw a real-life gunfighter."

"Wow."

"Inside, children," Appo said. "Let's take this inside."

Ben heard Bethany leave her room, walk down the hall, and knock on his door, but he didn't answer. He was doing just what Bethany said he was doing, sulking.

He hated when Ma slapped him, and he hated it when she did it in front of Bethany. But there was nothing he could do about it. She was his ma.

And despite what Bethany said, she was the only

ma she had ever known. Ben didn't know how Bethany could disrespect her so. Ma was a strong woman who ran her own business, and was successful at it. She knew what she was doing. He wished she and Bethany got along better, so Bethany could learn more from her.

And Ma was right about one thing: Despite the fact that she was his half sister, Ben loved Bethany. He was *in* love with her, but he knew Bethany would never look at him the same way.

Maybe Ma was right.

Maybe he was sick.

FIFTEEN

True to her word, Angie made sure Clint had the best dish in the house—beef stew. And she kept the cold beer coming, too.

"Ready for dessert?" she said when she picked up his clean plate.

"I'm ready for some pie."

"Oh," she said. "Okay, pie first, and then dessert."

He wasn't sure if she was just flirting with him, or if she really wanted something more. He watched her with the other patrons, and while they all seemed to be following her cleavage, she did not seem to be giving them the attention she was giving him. Not that this was something new to him. He'd had connections with many women right from their first meeting, and often it ended up with them in bed.

He was hoping that this was one of those times.

"Wait a minute," Red said when Bethany was in the middle of her story. "Tall with a scar on his cheek—here?" He touched his own face.

"That's right."

"That's the Gunsmith?"

"Well, yeah . . ."

Red looked at Appo.

"The man I told you about in the station? The one who caught me? That was him."

"He caught you?" Bethany asked, eyes widening.

"Now wait," Appo said. "You can't be sure it was the same man."

"He had a gun on him," Red said. "He had it in his belt in the back. I felt it."

Appo looked at Bethany, who was staring back with frightened eyes.

"Did you have any contact with this man?"

"No!" she said. "I wanted to try . . . but I didn't have time."

"Could he be connected with this woman who was killed?"

"I don't know," she said.

Appo rubbed his jaw.

"That'd be one hell of a coincidence."

"Red's gotta be wrong," Bethany said.

"Why would Captain Byrnes be meeting this man at the station?" Appo asked. He was talking to himself more than to the two young people with him. "The man would have to be someone of substance."

"Like the Gunsmith!" Red said.

"Red," Appo said, "you put the word out on the street. I want to know what hotel the captain has put this man up at."

"I can do that."

"George," Bethany said, "if it is the Gunsmith—"

"It may just be a coincidence that he's here, Bethany."

"But you don't believe in coincidences, George."

"No, you're right, girl," Appo said. "I don't."

The pie and coffee at the tavern were excellent. Clint didn't know how the hotel was going to be, but the captain had put him next to a good place to drink and eat.

Angie came over and poured him some more coffee, bending over so that her breasts were nice and close to him.

"You keep doing that," he said, "and I'm just going to have to take you up to my room with me."

She stood up straight, put one hand on her hip, and said, "I thought you'd never ask."

She walked away then, leaving him unsure whether or not she was kidding.

He finished his coffee and when she came over with his bill, he paid it.

"You goin' right back to your room?" she asked.

"I thought I'd have a beer at the bar first."

"That's good," she said. "I get off in about half an hour. Unless you were kiddin' about takin' me to your room?"

"Uh, no, I wasn't kidding," he said. "I just didn't know if, uh—"

"I wasn't kiddin'," she said. "I took to you right off, mister, and I don't like to waste time. If you don't like women like that, let me know now; it'll save us a lot of trouble."

"No trouble, Angie," Clint said. "I'll just sit at the bar with a beer and wait for you. To tell you the truth,

I've been on a train a long time. I need to do something that'll use a little energy."

"Oh, honey," she said, "for me you're gonna need a lot of energy."

SIXTEEN

The only one who couldn't wait to get her breasts out of that peasant blouse even more than Clint was Angie herself.

The impressive orbs bobbed free as she lifted the blouse over her head. While her arms were still in the air, Clint buried his face between the luscious globes. The scent was even more heady with his nose pressed against her. There were no more keys, there was nothing between them than more of Angie herself.

Her nipples were pink and erect, and as Clint had predicted, the size of a puppy's nose. He suckled them lovingly, then bit them, causing her to squeal.

"Wow, you're anxious," she said.

He pulled his face away from her flesh long enough to say, "From the moment I walked into the tavern."

"Well, that works both ways," she said. "My nipples don't ever get that hard—no, that's a lie. They do. I'm a girl who loves sex and I ain't shy about it. I know most women don't talk about it like I do—except maybe whores."

"You're talking an awful lot right now, Angie," Clint said. "Did you come here to talk?"

"No," she said, reaching for his trousers. "I sure enough came here to fuck."

She yanked his pants down, but stopped when she got them over his hips.

"You ain't one of them men who's gonna fall in love with me, are you?"

"Maybe for a few days," he said, "but that's all. I promise."

"Good enough." She yanked his pants and underwear down so that his erect penis fairly popped free. Her eyes got big and she said, "Ahhh."

Once she got rid of his boots, she was able to toss the pants and underwear away. That done, she fondled his balls with one hand and took his cock in the other. Holding it steady she first licked the head, getting it good and wet, then ran her tongue down it until she could lick his balls. She licked her way back up to the tip, then popped it into her mouth and slid him halfway into her mouth.

Letting him slide out, glistening with her saliva, she said, "I knew you were gonna taste just like candy."

Her frank talk excited him almost as much as her naked skin. Almost, but not quite. He wanted to see more of her.

"Let's get that skirt off," he said.

They did so together. When her wide hips and full butt came into view, he was fully and completely impressed with Angie.

The other thing that was impressive was the heat that came off her. It was as if her skin were on fire from the inside.

He wondered what else was on fire.

• • •

Appo, Red, and Bethany came out of the Metropole. Appo stopped to light a cigar.

"Red, you better get to work on that information," Appo said.

"Right, George. See you, Miss Bethany."

The kid ran off.

Bethany said, "You put a lot of faith in that boy, George."

"That boy's got more connections in Five Points than anybody I know—except me."

"Still . . ."

"And I trust him as much as I trust you."

"That much?"

"Well, maybe not that much."

They walked down the steps and started strolling.

"When are you gonna get away from that crazy woman?" Appo asked.

"As soon as I can convince Ben."

"That shouldn't be too hard," Appo said, looking at her. "He's in love with you."

"He's my brother, George."

"Half brother," George said, "but he's still in love with you. All you'd have to do to convince him is—"

"Oh, George," Bethany said. "I know what you're gonna say, and that's awful. He's my brother, half or not."

"How bad do you want to get him away from that woman?" Appo asked.

"She's his mother, George," Bethany said. "That's a hard connection to break."

"Not if she was my mother," George said.

"Well . . . I don't know what to do. I think she'll be

the death of him, George. Her or that crazy Willie O'Donnell."

"Him," Appo said. "I can have him killed if you like. I've told you that before."

"You wouldn't kill him yourself, would you, George?" she asked.

"No, no," Appo said, "but I can have it done."

"I couldn't do that, George."

"No, but I could."

"I'd feel responsible," she said, shaking her head. "No, I couldn't do that."

"Well," Appo said, "suit yourself."

Byrnes finished up some paperwork on his desk as Sergeant Bill O'Halloran came into his office.

"What have you got for me, Bill?"

"Not much, Cap'n," O'Halloran said. "No word on the street about haul that big comin' in."

"Not yet, maybe," Byrnes said. "Keep your ear to the ground, Sergeant."

"Yes, sir."

O'Halloran left and Byrnes sat back in his chair. If Clint Adams was right, somebody would be pulling into New York in a few days with two or three wagons full of goods. They might just have to wait and see who it was instead of trying to figure it out ahead of time.

He wondered if a man with the reputation of the Gunsmith could stay out of trouble for that long. It would make Talbot Roper very unhappy if Byrnes let his friend get killed.

SEVENTEEN

Clint found Angie to be a handful of woman—in fact, many handfuls. And he loved having some of her in each hand.

Lying on his back with his hard cock buried deep inside her, he had one of her big breasts in each hand, thumbing those big nipples. She bit her lower lip and rode him up and down with her hands pressed down on his belly for balance.

"Ooh, God, Clint," she moaned. "You sure do give a gal a good ride."

"I'm only giving as good as I get," he assured her.

"Mmm," she said, closing her eyes and bouncing up and down on him even harder . . .

Later he had his hands full with her butt, one cheek in each as he fucked her from behind, sliding his cock up between her smooth thighs and into her hot, steamy pussy. With every thrust into her, she pushed back against him so that their flesh made a slapping sound. It was a sound he'd heard many times before. It generally meant he was doing something right, and something that felt good, and this time that went double.

He admired the line of her back while he fucked her, and the way her muscles moved beneath her skin. She was a well-padded woman, but also well-muscled. She told him she was Irish, and the way Irish women ate was why she was well-padded. He told her he didn't mind a little extra meat on a woman, not at all, and he was proving it.

The bed creaked beneath them as they both grunted with the effort they were expending.

He pulled free of her reluctantly, but only long enough to turn her over. Once she was on her back and he could see those fine breasts, he slid his dick back into her before it could cool off. He was fascinated by the way her breasts jiggled and bounced as he drove into her.

"If I was a smaller gal, my teats wouldn't be bouncin' around this way," she told him.

"They're bouncing around just fine, Angie."

"You really do like you a good-sized woman, don't you?"

"I like all women, Angie," he admitted to her. "Big, small, it doesn't matter. You've all got something beautiful about you."

She wrapped her thighs around him tightly and said, "Maybe I can prove there's something more about me than all the others."

"You're sure welcome to try."

Later he stroked her flesh as they lay close together. He felt the fullness of her breasts, the curve of her hips, the swell of her belly, the softness of the blond hair between her legs, and the smoothness of her wet pussy lips.

"Mmm," she said. "You're gonna get me all hot and bothered again, Clint."

"Can't say I'd mind if that was the case, Miss . . . What is your last name?" he asked. "All you told me is that you're Irish."

"O'Doul," she said, "of the Five Points O'Douls."

"Five Points," he said. "That's a pretty rough neighborhood hereabouts, isn't it?"

"It is, and it's where I grew up."

"How did you grow up so sweet, then?" he asked.

"I had lots of brothers who kept me safe," she said. "Bein' safe made me sweet, I guess."

"And what happened to those brothers?"

"There was five of them," she said. "Three of them didn't make it out of Five Points."

"Dead?"

"Before they were twenty."

"And the other two?"

"They're still around."

"I shouldn't be expecting a visit from them after tonight, should I?"

She laughed and rubbed his chest.

"Not unless you hurt my feelin's," she said. "And you ain't done that yet."

"No yet about it," he said. "I have no intention of hurting your feelings."

"So if I was to do this," she asked, rolling over on top of him, flattening her big breasts against his chest and reaching between them to grab ahold of him, "you wouldn't object?"

"Not at all."

"And if I did this?" She shifted her hips and slid him inside her. "You wouldn't object?" Her voice had gotten a lot huskier.

"No," he said, with a sigh, "can't say as I would."

"Mmm," she said, kissing him lightly on the lips. "Then I don't think we'll be needin' to tell my brothers about this at all."

EIGHTEEN

The next morning Clint woke with Angie lying on his left arm. He leaned over and kissed her shoulder and breathed in the scent of her hair, but she didn't stir. He didn't blame her. They'd tired each other out pretty well the night before.

He slid his arm from beneath her and got out of bed. At the window he looked down at the street. The sun was out, but just barely, so it was probably just after six. He decided to let her sleep. She probably didn't have to go to work until later. He washed up in the basin as quietly as he could, then got dressed and left the room. He was wearing a jacket so he could continue to wear the New Line in his belt, out of sight.

In the small lobby he found a different clerk at the desk.

"I'm in room fifteen," he told the young man. "Adams."

"Oh, yes, Mr. Adams," the clerk said. "I know about you. Welcome."

"Thanks. Is there a place within walking distance where I can get a good breakfast?"

"About two blocks, just past the telegraph office," the clerk said.

"Okay, thanks."

"My name's Ted, Mr. Adams. You need anything, you just ask Owen or me."

"I'll do that."

As Clint started to leave, the clerk called, "Oh, how stupid of me."

"What's wrong?" Clint asked.

"I mentioned the telegraph office and then I forgot to give you this."

Clint walked back and accepted the telegram Ted was holding out to him.

"You were waiting for this, weren't you?"

"Yes, I was."

"Came in late last night."

"Telegraph office is open that late?"

"The clerk Len, he brought it over after he closed. He does that sometimes."

"Well, I'm much obliged," Clint said.

He took the telegram out onto the street with him before he opened it and read it. Bat Masterson promised to try his best to come up with something, but reminded Clint that he wasn't a detective. Not even "one in training, like you."

Smiling, Clint folded the telegram and put it in his pocket. He started down the street toward the telegraph office, and beyond it to the restaurant the clerk had told him about, but he knew immediately he was being followed. Between the telegraph office and the restaurant he quickly stepped into a doorway and waited. Soon, his tail passed by. Clint stepped out and picked him up off his feet.

"Lemme go, lemme go," the kid yelled. "Put me down, I tell ya!"

"Are you going to talk to mc?"

"Yeah, yeah, okay."

He put the kid down and turned him around and found himself looking into the face of the young pickpocket Red.

"You."

"Yeah, it's me."

"Why are you following me?"

"I was wonderin' if you needed any help yet, mister?" Red asked.

"Maybe you were hoping for another chance at my wallet?"

"Oh, no, sir," Red said. "I was just hopin' to make some money off ya—ya know, help ya out."

"Well, I could use some help, now that you mention it," Clint said.

"That's great. What do I gotta do?"

"You can help me eat some breakfast."

NINETEEN

"How did you find me?" Clint asked.

Red was sitting across the table from him, a full plate of bacon and eggs and potatoes laid out in front of him. The same was in front of Clint, which gave the kid a man-sized appetite.

"I got connections," the boy said. "I found out that the cap'n took you to the Belvedere Hotel. I was just waitin' for ya out front."

"How long?"

"I came at first light."

Clint picked up a forkful of eggs and bacon and shoveled it in. There was never any shortage of good food in New York, that he remembered well.

"What do you do with yourself all day, Red?" Clint asked.

"I pick pockets."

"That's it?"

"That's all I can do until I grow up."

"And then what?"

The boy's face lit up.

"When I grow up, I'm goin' on the con."

"You ever go to school?"

"Naw," he said.

"What about your parents?"

"Been dead since I was little."

"So where do you live?"

"Here and there," Red said. "Mostly around Five Points."

"That's a pretty rough neighborhood for a kid, isn't it?"

"Not if you was born there," Red said. "Everybody in Five Points is my friends."

"Well, that's good," Clint said. "It's good to have a lot of friends."

"Yeah, it sure is."

Red kept feeding his face while he talked, and before long his plate was empty while Clint's was still half full.

"You full?" Clint asked.

"Not hardly."

"You want some more?"

"Sure."

"Well, you can have some."

"Swell."

"As soon as you tell me why you're really here," Clint said. "Why you were really looking for me."

"I tol' ya," Red said. "I was just tryin' to make some money from ya."

Clint studied the boy for a few moments, still convinced that he was lying, but he waved the waiter over anyway.

"Bring the boy another order," Clint said. "Same thing."

"Yes, sir."

The waiter looked at Red, made a face as if the smell was too much to bear, and then left.

"When's the last time you had a bath?" Clint asked.

"I ain't done nothin'," the boy said. "Why do I need a bath."

"It's not a punishment."

"It ain't?"

"Being clean is no punishment, Red."

"I ain't got time to be clean," the boy said. "I got work to do. If I don't pick pockets, I don't eat . . . and I never eat as good as this."

"Well then, I guess you better stock up."

"Thanks, mister . . . What's yer name?"

"Adams," Clint said. "My name is Clint Adams."

Red stared at him.

"It is?"

"Yes."

"But . . . ain't you the Gunsmith?"

"I suppose so."

Red sat forward. "I read about you in Mr. Buntline's dime novels."

Clint knew about those novels. They hadn't done him any good.

"You can't believe everything you read."

"I know how to read!"

"I don't doubt that," Clint said. "Take it easy. I know you can read. I'm just saying don't believe everything."

"You mean Mr. Buntline lies?"

"Let's just say he exaggerates a bit."

"Well," Red said, "even if half what I read is right, well . . . you're a legend."

"Don't be so quick to be impressed, Red," Clint

said as the waiter brought another plate and put it in front of the boy. "Why don't you just eat up?"

Red's eyes widened at the new plate of food and he said, "All right!"

TWENTY

After breakfast Clint and Red stepped outside the restaurant.

"I sure do thank you for the grub, Mr. Adams," Red said.

"Just call me Clint, Red."

"Okay, Clint."

"Where are you off to now, Red?"

"I got business, Clint." The boy pulled on a dirty cap. "I got business every day."

"Pickpocket business?"

"That's right."

"Aren't you afraid of being arrested?"

Red grinned.

"The police can't catch me, I'm too fast."

"I caught you."

"Yeah, but you're the Gunsmith. Well, I gotta get goin'."

"Hold on."

"For what?" Red asked, squinting up at Clint.

Clint put his hand in his pocket. "I just want to make sure I've still got my wallet."

"Aw . . ."

Appo frowned at the knock on his door. He had just poured himself a cup of coffee and carried it to the door with him.

"Red," Appo said. "What brings you around here this early?"

"Ain't so early, George," Red said. "I been up for hours."

"Come on in, then."

Red entered and Appo closed the door.

"You want some breakfast?"

"Had some."

"Well, it couldn't've been much—"

"Two plates of bacon, eggs, and spuds," Red said proudly.

"Wow, you must've had a big hit."

"The biggest."

Appo regarded the boy over the rim of his coffee cup, then said, "Well, okay, you're busting to tell me."

"I had breakfast with the Gunsmith."

"Then it was him?"

"Yep."

"All I asked you to do was find out what hotel he was in, Red."

"I did," Red said, "but I wanted to make sure it was the same man, so I went and had a look myself."

"And . . . ?"

"He caught me followin' him."

"Well, this fella must be good," Appo said. "He's caught you twice."

"He's the Gunsmith, George," Red said. "He's a legend."

"So I hear," Appo said. He was pretty used to being on the receiving end of all of Red's adoration, so he was feeling a tingle of jealousy as the boy talked about Clint Adams.

"Well, I guess it's not such a coincidence that he's here in New York," Appo said.

"He musta come lookin' for Bethany and Ben, huh?" Red asked.

"It's more likely he doesn't know who he's looking for, Red," Appo said. "It's probably Willie, since he's the one who killed that woman."

"The Gunsmith is lookin' fer a killer?" Red asked. "But he ain't a detective."

"Apparently that doesn't matter. Red, what hotel is he staying at?"

"The Belvedere."

"A favorite hideaway of Captain Byrnes when he has a dignitary in town," Appo said. "I think there is also a telegraph office a block or two from there."

"Sure is. We passed it while we was walking to the restaurant."

"Well," Appo said, "maybe I ought to have a talk with the clerk there."

"You think the Gunsmith sent a telegram to somebody?" Red asked.

"That's what I'm going to find out, my boy," Appo said.

"I'll go with you," Red said.

"No," Appo said. "You're no good to me now when it comes to Adams. He's seen you twice. And, obviously, he's fed you."

"Really well!"

"Then I suppose he's managed to earn himself one fan in town," Appo said.

"Don't worry, George," Red said. "To me you're still the greatest."

TWENTY-ONE

When Bethany came out the next morning, she found Ben sitting on the front steps. She sat down next to him and bumped his shoulder with hers. She loved him dearly, but as a brother. She wished that was enough for him.

"Hey," she said.

"Hey, yourself."

"Still sulking?"

"Naw," he said, "I'm over that. Now I'm just angry."

"Jesus, Ben," she said, "you're always angry."

"Yeah, I know," he said. "I feed on it."

"I think it feeds on you," she said.

"I'm gonna have to go and see Ma today," Ben said. "You wanna come?"

"No," she said. "I never like to see her unless I have to. And I don't want to see how she treats you. When do you figure Willie will get here with the goods?"

"Another few days, at least," he said.

"Good," she said. "The longer I go without seein' his ugly face the better."

"You and me both. You see George last night?"

"Yeah. I ate with him and Little Red at the Metropole."

"That little guy's got a bad crush on you," he said.

She nudged him with her elbow and said, "That makes two of you, huh?"

He leaned away from her.

"Don't tease me, Bethany. You know how I feel about you."

"I do know, Ben," she said, "and I try to make light of it. It ain't right. You're my brother."

"Half brother."

"Still . . ."

"I'm sorry," he said. "It's just how I feel."

"You have to find a nice girl, Ben."

"Bethany," he asked, "what would a nice girl want with me?"

Clint approached the clerk at the front desk and had to admit to himself he didn't know if it was Owen or Ted.

"Hello."

The young man looked up. It was Ted, the one from earlier in the morning.

"You said if I needed anything," Clint said. "Did you mean . . . anything?"

Ted looked around, then leaned on the desk and lost the benign look he'd been wearing.

"Yes, sir . . . *anything*. Are you in need of . . . something special?"

"Not as special as what you're thinking," Clint replied.

"I didn't think so," Ted said. "I saw Angie leave a little while ago."

"Yes, well, what I need is a message delivered to someone who lives in Brooklyn," Clint said, "on Sackett Street. His name is Delvecchio."

"Just Delvecchio?"

"That's all he goes by."

"What's the message, sir?"

"That I'm here, and would like to see him."

"That's it?"

"That's all."

"You wouldn't want him . . . brought here?"

"No," Clint said. He took a couple dollars from his pocket and laid them on the desktop. "Just deliver the message today."

"Yes, sir." Ted slid the money from the desk into his pocket.

"Thank you."

"Not at all, sir," Ted said, once again assuming that blank, benign look he and Owen shared when it suited them.

Clint left the hotel and wondered what his next move should be. Delvecchio was a private detective who lived in Brooklyn. He and Clint had worked together the last time he'd been in New York. The detective had helped him with Teddy Roosevelt, Annie Oakley, and P. T. Barnum. No such names involved this time, but maybe the man would still be willing to help.

He was going to be interested in Delvecchio's opinion of Captain Tom Byrnes. He already knew that Delvecchio respected Talbot Roper's reputation—a rep supported by Clint himself. Well, Clint respected the Brooklyn detective's opinions, so a conversation about Byrnes would be very interesting.

Clint decided to go down to Printers Row to spend some time in one of the newspaper morgues. He wanted to do some reading about the fencing and pickpocket situation in Manhattan.

TWENTY-TWO

Captain Thomas Byrnes came into his office that morning, refreshed from a good night's sleep. He called O'Halloran into his office immediately.

"What have you got for me?" he asked.

"Sir?"

"On those fences."

"Sir . . . I've only just come in."

"You didn't work on it last night?"

"Uh, no, sir."

"Did you give it any thought at all?"

"Uh, yes, sir."

"And what conclusions have you come up with?"

"Sir?"

"Sergeant," Byrnes said patiently, "give me the names of three fences you think could handle as much merchandise as we are talking about."

"Uh, yes, sir," O'Halloran said, thinking fast. "Buzzy Rothstein, Declan Murphy, and . . . Ma Mandelbaum.

"Good," Byrnes said. He wrote down the three names. "Keep your ear to the ground, Sergeant."

"Yes, sir."

As O'Halloran left and closed his boss's door behind him, Byrnes sat back. He'd thought of Fredericka Mandelbaum himself. This was the kind of thing she'd do to make a point that she was as good or better than the men in the business.

Yes, he should probably have a talk with the Queen of Fences, but first a check to see how Clint Adams was doing.

Bethany was still sitting on the front steps, worrying about Ben when Red came along and plopped himself right next to her.

"Hi, Bethany."

"Hello, Red."

"You look sad."

"I've got things on my mind, Red."

"What things?"

"Grown-up things," she said. "You wouldn't understand."

"Well, I got somethin' I think might cheer ya up."

"Oh, yeah? What's that?"

"Clint Adams."

"What about him?"

"That was him I saw in the train station."

"How do you know?"

He told her about having breakfast with the Gunsmith that morning.

"You better not be lying to me, Red."

"I ain't lyin', I swear, Bethany," Red said. "I wouldn't lie to you."

"You'd lie to your mother, if she was alive," Bethany pointed out.

"I know," he said, "but not to you."

She studied him for a few moments, then asked, "Now, why would that be good news to me? If he's in New York, it means he's lookin' for whoever killed that woman in Denver."

"And that wasn't you, right?"

"Right."

"So then he ain't lookin' for you," Red said. "Ain't that good news?"

"That's right," she said. "He's lookin' for Willie O'Donnell."

"Right."

"But . . ."

"But what?"

She turned and patted Red on the head.

"Never mind, Red," she said. "Thanks a lot."

"You want me to leave, don't ya?"

She smiled at him. "I have some thinking to do."

"Grown-up thinkin', right?"

"Right."

"Okay," he said, standing up. He took his cloth hat from his pocket and jammed it on his head. "Ya don't gotta tell me twice."

As Red walked away, Bethany started to worry about Ben again. It wasn't Willie who people might have seen with Libby Wellington in Denver—it was Ben. People were bound to remember the handsome young man who was hanging around the older woman in the last days before she was killed.

What if Clint Adams was in New York looking for Ben?

She sprang off the steps and ran down the block after Red.

"Hey, Red," she said, grabbing his shoulder.

"Don't do that!" Red said, turning around. "You scared the crap outta me."

"I'm sorry, I'm sorry," she said. "Look, where did you say Clint Adams was staying?"

"The Belvedere Hotel," Red said. "Union Square."

"Thanks, Red, thanks." She turned and started running.

"Crazy girls!" Red said.

TWENTY-THREE

Clint came out of the morgue of the the *Morning Tele-graph* with black ink on his hands. He'd been through the morgue copies of the paper and now knew that Captain Tom Byrnes had been a bear on pickpockets in New York in recent months, and in recent years had been the main reason for the increase in proficiency of the New York City Police Department. Byrnes, from what Clint could glean from the newspapers—and from reading between the lines—was both feared and respected by the lowlifes of New York.

Clint wanted a drink, but first he wanted to wash the ink from his hands. He decided to go back to the hotel, wash up, and then get that drink at the tavern next door.

"Anyone looking for me?" Clint asked the clerk. Damn. Couldn't tell if it was Owen or Ted.

"No, sir. No one asked, and no one has been looking. Oh, and we got that message delivered for you."

"Thank you."

He went upstairs, washed his hands, and then came back down to go to the tavern. As he entered, he spot-

ted both Angie and Captain Thomas Byrnes. One of
them smiled at him, and the other waved.

Since Byrnes was at his table, Clint joined him.
Angie hurried over to take his order.

"Beer, please, Angie," he said. "A cold one."

"Comin' right up."

The captain already had half a beer in front of him,
so he waved her away.

"I thought I might find you here," Byrnes said.
"Wanted to check on your progress."

"Not much," Clint said, "except to become more
impressed with you."

Byrnes wiped some beer foam from his mustache
with his finger and said, "What's that?"

"I checked the morgue at the *Telegraph*—went
back quite a few months. Seems you're making it hard
for the criminal element in New York to make a living."

"That's just my job," Byrnes said.

"Nevertheless, it's impressive. Think if I stay away
a couple of years again and then come back, the streets
will be clean of crime."

"Not much chance of that," Byrnes said, "but it's a
nice thought."

"What about you?" Clint asked. "Any luck?"

"I can think of two or three fences who might be
able to handle the volume of merchandise we're talking about," Byrnes said. "I'm going to talk to them."

"Mind if I come along?" Clint asked. "Looks like I
don't have that much to do until the stuff gets here."

"I'm going to go and see Ma Mandelbaum down in
Little Italy right from here," Byrnes said. "Don't see
any reason why you shouldn't tag along."

"Can I have a drink first?" Clint asked. "Kind of dry in that morgue."

"Sure," Byrnes said. "There's no hurry."

Angie brought Clint his beer, set it down, and made sure she bumped him with her hip as she was leaving. Byrnes noticed, but said nothing.

"I sent a message to a friend of mine," Clint said. "Thought he might be of some help."

"Bat Masterson, you mean?"

"No," Clint said, "not that message. I sent one here in town. Well, to Brooklyn, actually."

"Brooklyn?" Byrnes said it as if it were some foreign country he hated. "What's this friend's name?"

"Delvecchio," Clint said. "He's a private—"

"I know who Delvecchio is, Mr. Adams."

Clint wondered what happened to "Clint"?

"I would think you'd pick your friends a little more carefully."

"He's been a big help to me during my other visits," Clint said. "What's your problem with him?"

"He plays both sides," Byrnes said. "In my book you've got to pick a side. If you don't, then you might as well be bent."

Clint didn't say anything. Byrnes seemed real intense about this, and Clint didn't want to get on the man's bad side. He also didn't want to insult Talbot Roper's friend.

"I'll keep that in mind, Captain."

Byrnes finished his beer, wiped away the foam again, then seemed to relax.

"I'm sorry," he said. "I don't mean to tell you who your friends should be. It's just . . . if I were you, I'd be careful of Mr. Delvecchio. That's all I'm saying."

"I appreciate it, Captain," Clint said. "I mean it, I'll keep your words in mind."

"You finish your beer," Byrnes said. "I want to talk to the bartender a moment. Then we'll go and see Ma Mandelbaum. She is known as the Queen of Fences."

"Sounds like somebody who's going to be interesting to meet," Clint said.

"Interesting is the least of it," Byrnes said.

TWENTY-FOUR

Bethany got to the Belvedere Hotel just in time to see Clint Adams leave and go to the tavern next door. When she hurried over and peered in the window, she saw him joining Captain Byrnes at a table. There was no way she could go in and talk to him, not while he was with Byrnes.

She was just going to have to wait.

Clint finished his beer as Byrnes came walking back over.

"You ready to go meet the only female fence in Manhattan?" Byrnes asked.

"I'm ready."

He stood up and the two men walked to the door. Clint waved at Angie and signaled to her that he'd see her later. At least, he hoped she understood what he was trying to convey. Either way, she smiled and blew him a kiss.

Outside, Clint saw the captain's carriage pull up. The driver must have been down the street. How he knew they were coming out was anybody's guess.

When they climbed in, Byrnes knocked on the side of the carriage and the driver took off, obviously aware of what their next stop was supposed to be.

"Tell me about this lady fence," Clint said.

"Fredericka Mandelbaum . . ." Byrnes started.

Bethany watched the two men climb into the police carriage and then watched it pull away. She had no idea where it was going, and she wasn't up to running after it. She decided to stay at the hotel and wait for Clint Adams to come back. She had to talk to him about Ben . . . and about Willie.

The carriage stopped on the corner of Clinton and Rivington streets, in front of the dry goods store that Fredericka Mandelbaum's husband, Wolf, used to own and run. Since his death his wife ran it as a front—or so Byrnes said—for a fencing operation.

"If you know that, why not close her down?" Clint asked during the ride.

"We can never catch her red-handed."

"Maybe stopping in unexpectedly like this might do it."

"I doubt it," Byrnes said. "But one can hope."

They got out and approached the store, which had a Closed sign on the door.

"Closed this early?"

"Ma makes her own hours," Byrnes said. "That sign gets turned around more times in one day than . . . well, a lot."

Byrnes knocked, then knocked harder.

"Does she live here, too?" Clint asked.

"Upstairs."

This time Byrnes pounded on the door. Eventually, the door was opened by a young man.

"Hello, Ben."

"Captain Byrnes," the boy said. Clint figured him for about twenty, slender and handsome.

"Clint, this is Ben. He's Ma's son. Ben, this is Clint Adams."

"What's that to me?"

Byrnes smiled and looked at Clint.

"Ben's a tough guy," he said. "Or wants to be. Where's Ma, Ben?"

"She don't wanna see you," the boy said.

"Since when does she have a choice?" Byrnes pushed the door open, forcing the boy back. He and Clint stepped into the store. "Tell Ma we're here."

Ben stood his ground for a full five seconds, then turned and went through a curtained doorway in the back.

"Looks like a regular dry goods store," Clint said.

"It is, when it's open," Byrnes said. "Ma needs to keep it running. She needs the front, the set of books. She's got to show a loss."

The curtain opened and a woman stepped through. She was a hard-looking woman in her fifties. She wore her hair in a bun, but the style was too old for her. With a little help, Clint thought, she'd be attractive.

"What the hell do you want, Byrnes?" she demanded.

Her voice was rough, gravelly. There was nothing she could do about that. In a more attractive package the voice would be even more startling.

"Hello, Ma. Nice to see you."

"Like hell," she said. "I always hate seein' you."

Ben came out of the back, stood behind his mother. "Who's your handsome friend?"

"This is Clint Adams."

Ma Mandelbaum looked at Clint.

"Say, I know that name," she said. "You're a big deal out West, ain'tcha? Yeah, I know you. The Gunsmith." She turned and looked at Ben. "This here's the Gunsmith, Ben. You better treat him with some respect or he'll take out his six-gun and shoot us." She turned back to Clint. "You gonna shoot us, Mr. Gunsmith?"

"Not in front of the captain," Clint said. "Maybe I'll come back later and do it."

Ma stared at him for a few moments, then burst out laughing.

TWENTY-FIVE

"What brings you around here, Captain?" Ma asked. "You wanna search my place again?"

"I heard Ben was out of town, Ma," Byrnes said. "When did he get back?"

"Yesterday. What of it?"

"Didn't happen to be in Denver, did he?"

"Why don't you ask Ben?"

"Because Ben's a tough guy," Byrnes said. "He wouldn't answer me. Would you, Ben?"

"What do you think?"

"See?" Byrnes looked at Clint. "Tough guy."

"I see."

"There's your tough guy," Ma said, pointing at Clint. "He's the gunfighter, the killer."

"He hasn't killed anybody in New York," Byrnes said. "Yet."

"Why don't you and your hired gun get outta my place?" Ma said.

"We're looking for some goods, Ma," Byrnes said. "Coming in from the West. You know anything about it?"

"Why would I?"

"You're one of the only fences in town who could handle that much merchandise, Ma. What do you say? Want to confess?"

"To what? I run a dry goods store, that's all."

"Where's Bethany? Maybe we should talk to her."

"You leave her alone," Ben snapped.

"Who's Bethany?" Clint asked.

"Just a stupid girl," Ma said.

"Bethany is Ben's sister," Byrnes said.

"Half sister," Ma said.

"Only Ben's in love with her," Byrnes went on. "What do you think of that? In love with his own sister."

"Why don't you shut up!"

"Go in the back, Ben," Ma said. "Go ahead. Shoo."

Reluctantly, Ben did what his mother said.

"You going to keep that boy a mama's boy his whole life, Ma?"

"Why don't you go bother somebody else, Captain?" she demanded.

"I intend to. I'm going to go bother your competitors. I just thought I'd start bothering you first."

"Well, you did a good job. Ya ruined the rest of my day."

"Well, Ma," Byrnes said with a smile, "that just makes mine."

Outside, Clint said, "She's a rough customer."

"The roughest," Byrnes said.

"What about the boy?"

"He tries to be rough for her, but he's not. He just hasn't got it in him."

"And that thing about his sister? Bethany?"

"That was true," Byrnes said. "Ma doesn't like the girl very much, but Ben does love her—but not as a sister."

"And Bethany?"

"Oh, to her he's just her brother. She loves him, but as a brother. Come on. I'll take you back to your hotel."

"About those other competitors?"

"Yeah, I'm going to talk to them tomorrow."

"Can I tag along then, too?"

"Sure, why not?" Byrnes said. "Come on, I'll fill you in on them in the carriage."

When Ben came out of the back room, Ma slapped him across the face.

"What was that for?" he demanded.

"That was for lettin' them in," she said. "Where's that girl?"

"She's home."

"Well, get 'er. I don't want Byrnes or that Adams talkin' to her."

"What's Adams doin' here?" Ben asked. "He's a gunman from the West."

"Well, somehow he tracked you two here," Ma Mandelbaum said. "You musta messed up somewhere."

"Not us," he said. "He didn't track us."

"We'll see about that," Ma said. "You get that wretched girl and bring her back here."

"She ain't wretched."

"You wanna get slapped again? Don't back talk me, just go and get 'er!"

Ben stared at her, tried to hold his ground, but in the end he said, "Yes, Ma."

TWENTY-SIX

Byrnes let Clint out in front of his hotel. It was just starting to get dark.

"Long day," Clint said.

"I'll pick you up in the morning, around eight. We'll go and see Rothstein and Murphy."

"I'll be ready."

The carriage pulled away. As Clint turned to enter the hotel, a girl suddenly blocked his way. She was young, pretty, scared, and trying not to show it.

"Bethany."

Her eyes widened.

"How did you—"

"I just came from seeing your mother."

"That's a joke," she said. "She doesn't act like a mother."

"I also saw Ben, your brother."

"My half brother."

"He's in love with you, isn't he?"

"Mr. Adams," she said, "I'm here to talk to you about my brother."

"All right," Clint said. "Would you like to come to my room?"

"Certainly not!"

"Okay," he said. "You're a nice girl—"

"There ain't nothin' nice about me," she said, "but I ain't goin' to your room."

"How about the tavern?"

"Tavern?"

"For coffee. You drink coffee, don't you?"

"Y-yes . . ."

"Okay, then," Clint said. "Let's go into the tavern and talk."

"All right."

Clint opened the door for her and let her go in ahead of him. The captain's table was empty, so he directed her to it. Angie came over immediately, her smile a little forced.

"Hello, Clint," she said. "Who's your friend?"

"Angie, this is Bethany," Clint said. "She wants to talk to me about her brother. Could we have two coffees?"

"Sure," she said. "Comin' up. Unless your friend wants somethin' stronger?"

"I don't drink."

"Sure you don't."

Angie went to get the coffee.

"Do you find her . . . pretty?" Bethany asked.

"Yes, I do."

"Hmph. You would."

"Bethany, you and Ben were in Denver, weren't you?" Clint asked.

"How did you find us here?" she asked.

"I wasn't looking for you, exactly," Clint said. "I'm looking for whoever killed Mrs. Wellington."

"Ben didn't do it," she said. "It was . . ."

"Come on, Bethany," Clint said. "If you're going to tell me who didn't do it, you have to tell me who did."

"I can't tell you why we were in Denver," she said. "I can't."

"I know why you were in Denver," Clint said. "You were there to get some goods for Ma to fence, right? Why'd she send you all the way to Denver for that?"

Angie came with their coffee.

"Sure you wouldn't rather have some milk and cookies, honey?" she asked.

"No, thank you. Coffee's fine."

Angie said to Clint, "Just wave if you need anything else."

"Look," Bethany said, "I—I only came to tell you that Ben didn't kill that woman. He wouldn't. He couldn't."

"He's too gentle, right?"

"Yes, that's right."

"I'll bet that makes Ma real mad."

"Furious. She loves him, I know that, but she's so mean to him, tryin' to toughen him up."

"And why doesn't she like you?"

"She didn't like my father, and she doesn't like me. But that doesn't matter."

"Do you love Ben, Bethany?"

"Yes, I do. He's my brother."

"Just as a brother?"

"Yes."

"How do you feel about the way he feels about you?"

"I'm sorry," she said. "I—I can't return those feelings."

"He'd do anything for you, wouldn't he?"

"Yes."

"Kill somebody?"

"No!"

"All right." Clint picked up his coffee cup, took a sip. Bethany ignored hers.

"What else?" Clint asked.

"That's it," she said. "He didn't do it."

"And I'm just supposed to believe you?"

"I hope so."

He sat back.

"You do believe me, don't you?"

"What do you do for a living, Bethany?"

"I—I pick pockets."

"And I'm supposed to believe what you say?"

"This only has to do with Ben, Mr. Adams," she said. "Please don't kill him."

"What makes you think I want to kill him?"

"Well, that's what you do, isn't it? Kill people? Isn't that who you are?"

"No, Bethany," Clint said, "that's not who I am. Is picking pockets who you are?"

"Unfortunately," she said, "yes. When you grow up in Five Points, there isn't much else."

"I met a kid from Five Points earlier today," he said. "Ten years old, black hair, but calls himself—"

"Red," she said. "I know him."

"That figures."

Suddenly, she stood up.

"I have to go."

"You know, Bethany," he said, "I'd find believing

you a lot easier if you told me who did kill the woman."

"I can't."

"I'm going to have to find out for myself then."

She shrugged and walked out. He let her go.

After a few minutes Angie came over and looked down at him.

"Your girlfriend left?"

"She's not my girlfriend," he said. "She's just a scared kid trying to help her brother."

"Sure. Hey, she didn't drink her coffee."

"I drank mine," Clint said, "but I could use a beer and some more of that beef stew."

"And then what?"

"And then, who knows?"

She smiled at him and said, "Okay."

She brought him a beer first and then went to get his supper.

Two kids had been sent to Denver by their mother to pick up some merchandise, and a woman got killed because of it. But Clint didn't believe there was any way Ben or Bethany could have killed Libby Wellington. That meant that Ma had sent somebody else with them. But who?

"Supper included in whatever job you got for me?"

Clint looked up and saw Delvecchio standing over him.

"You like beef stew?" Clint asked.

TWENTY-SEVEN

Delvecchio had a seat and Angie brought over two bowls of beef stew.

"Thank you, darlin'," Delvecchio said.

She gave him an extra long look at her breasts and then flounced off.

"How'd you find me?" Clint asked.

"Clerk over at the hotel told me to check over here," Delvecchio said. "He says they have somethin' over here you like. Is it her?"

"And the beef stew."

"It's good to see you, Clint."

"You, too, Delvecchio."

"What brings you to Manhattan? And what can I do for you?"

"I'll answer that while we eat," Clint said, "but I've got to tell you something. I'm also working with Captain Thomas Byrnes."

"Byrnes," Delvecchio said. "He hates me."

"I gathered that."

"You told him you sent me a message?"

"Yep."

"That was probably a bad move," the Brooklyn detective said, "but how could you have known that?"

"I couldn't," Clint said, "so if you're going to help me on this, you're going to have to stay away from him."

"I can do that," Delvecchio said. "I am getting paid, right?"

"Right."

"Then I can do that."

"Okay, then here's the story . . ."

"I know Ma Mandelbaum," Delvecchio said when Clint finished. "She is big enough to handle a haul like this. And the fact that Bethany came to you pretty much makes it a cinch that she's the fence."

"Means I probably won't have to go and see the other two with Byrnes tomorrow."

"Murphy and Rothstein? I know them, too. They could handle it, but they wouldn't have sent a couple of kids, along with whoever actually killed the woman."

"If you know the woman's operation," Clint asked, "do you have any ideas about that?"

"Sure," Delvecchio said. "Her current bed warmer is a guy named Willie O'Donnell. He'd kill a rich widow just as soon as look at her."

"Do you know if he's in town?"

"I'll check around tomorrow," Delvecchio said. "If he's not, then he's probably your guy. How you gonna get Byrnes to believe all this?"

"Why wouldn't he?"

"He takes his reputation very seriously," the other man said. "He probably won't be crazy about the fact that you cracked this case yourself."

"You mean I have to be careful of his ego?"

"I would."

"Roper didn't tell me he had one."

"Maybe Roper doesn't know," Delvecchio said. "After all, how often do they really see each other?"

"You've got a good point."

Delvecchio finished cleaning his bowl with a piece of bread, and then drained his beer mug.

"That was a helluva meal," he said. "I've gotta remember this place."

"You better remember something else, too."

"What's that?"

"Byrnes is a regular here."

"He is?"

Clint nodded. "In fact, this is his table."

Delvecchio peered across at Clint and asked, "You tryin' to get me killed? If he walked in here and saw me—"

"He dropped me off just before you got here," Clint said. "He's not coming back."

"Just to be on the safe side—I'm outta here." Delvecchio stood up.

Angie came running over, her breasts bobbing. "Leavin' so soon?"

"It pains me, darlin', but I gotta go. Clint, I'll be in touch."

Delvecchio put on the bowler hat he'd carried in with him, doffed it to her, and then left. Clint was going to have to ask him about the hat. He'd never known anyone who could make a bowler work other than Bat Masterson.

That reminded him. Maybe there was a telegram from Bat at the hotel desk for him.

"You got plans for the rest of the night?" Angie asked.

"I thought I'd just wait in my room for you to finish up here."

"Sure your little girlfriend won't be visitin' you?" she asked.

"Maybe I should go looking for her—"

"No, no," Angie said, "that's okay. I get off here in a few hours. Will you be awake?"

He smiled and said, "I'll be awake, and ready."

He entered the hotel lobby and went to the desk.

"Is there a telegram for me?" he asked.

"Sure is," Ted or Owen said. "Came in this afternoon." He handed it over.

"Thanks."

"Did, uh, your friend find you?"

"Yes, he did," Clint said. "Oh, and Angie from next door will be coming in later."

"I'll let her go right up."

"Thanks."

Clint took the telegram to his room and opened it when he was inside. According to Bat a young man had been seen in the company of Mrs. Wellington several times during the days before she died. According to Bat, he was, "tall, slender, a handsome lad."

Sure fit the description of Ben Mandelbaum to a T.

TWENTY-EIGHT

When Bethany got back to the rooming house that night, she knocked on Ben's door. He answered immediately. She could tell by the redness of his face that Ma had slapped him once or twice that day.

"Can I come in?"

He nodded, backed away.

"I went to see him today."

"Who?"

"The Gunsmith."

"Why did you do that, Bethany?" he demanded, grabbing her by the shoulders.

"I had to, Ben," she said. "I had to tell him that you didn't kill that woman."

"And did you tell him who did?"

"No."

"Well . . . it's good that you didn't," he said. "Tellin' him it was Willie would lead him right to Ma."

"Ben," she said, "I probably led him to Ma just by talkin' to him."

"Well," he said, "he came by to see Ma while I was there. He was with Captain Byrnes."

"What happened?"

"Nothin'. Ma talked her way out, like she always does."

"Sometimes I wish she wouldn't," Bethany said. "Sometimes I wish they'd just put her away."

"And then Willie would take over," Ben said. "That wouldn't help us at all."

He was still holding her by the shoulders, but more gently now. It made her uncomfortable.

"Ben, let me go."

Ben stared at her, but instead of letting her go he pulled her to him and kissed her, mashing his lips against hers. She pressed her lips tightly together and tried to pull away, but he was too strong. He didn't know how to kiss very well, but even if he did, he was her brother . . .

Finally, she managed to push away from him and catch her breath

"Ben Mandelbaum, don't you ever do that again."

"Bethany, I love you."

She turned, opened the door, and ran down the hall to her own room. She let herself in and locked the door behind her, then she wiped her lips with the back of her hand.

Alone in his room Ben cursed himself, then cursed his whole life. A mother like Ma, a half sister he had evil feelings for, a life that was going nowhere. Sometimes he just wanted to put a gun in his mouth and pull the trigger.

But he couldn't get the taste of his sister off his lips.

•   •   •

Later, there was a knock on Bethany's door. She

opened it cautiously. Ben was standing there looking contrite.

"I just wanted to tell you, Ma sent me to find you and bring you back."

"For what?"

"I don't know," he said. "It was after Adams and the captain left. She was mad, tol' me to go get you and bring you back to her."

"She probably wants to talk about Denver," Bethany said. "I don't want to talk about Denver. Let her get the story from Willie when he gets back. She's gonna believe his lies, anyway."

"What should I tell her?"

"Tell her she won't have to worry about me anymore," Bethany said. "Tell her I ain't comin' back."

"What are you gonna do, Bethany?" Ben asked. "How're you gonna make a livin'?"

"I'll talk to George," she said. "He'll help me."

"George Appo?" Ben asked. "He's too old for you!"

"I'm not gonna marry him, Ben," she said. "I'm just gonna ask him for help."

"And what do you think he's gonna want in return?" Ben asked. "He's a dirty old man—"

"He's not even ten years older than me. You're just jealous, Ben. It's . . . It's sick!"

"Bethany, don't—"

She slammed the door in his face, then buried her face in her hands and cried.

Ben left the building, shoulders slumped, wondering how Ma was going to react to the news.

• • •

Bethany listened at her door. When she was convinced that Ben had gone, she opened it, hurried down the hall, and ran out of the building.

TWENTY-NINE

Clint left the hotel the next morning with very little strength in his legs. If he spent every night with Angie, he wouldn't be able to walk at all by the time he was ready to leave New York. The woman had one of the most voracious sexual appetites he had ever run into.

There had been a message waiting for him at the front desk with Owen—or Ted. It was from Delvecchio, asking Clint to meet him for breakfast in a restaurant that was just a few blocks away on Broadway.

Clint found the restaurant to be small, clean, and doing a brisk business. It was, however, far different from the tavern, and not the kind of place Captain Byrnes would frequent. Delvecchio had already arrived and was seated at a back table.

"No chance of Byrnes runnin' into us here," the detective said.

"I agree."

They both ordered steak and eggs from a tired-looking, middle-aged waitress, then sat back with their coffee cups. Clint found the coffee weak, but said nothing.

"Why such an early meeting?" Clint asked.

"Too early for you? Did you have a rough night?" Delvecchio asked.

"No, I meant—"

"I know what you meant," the other man said. "How did I find something out so quickly? I didn't, really. I just did some quick checking on Mother Baum. Her man, Willie O'Donnell, is out of the city."

"Do we know where?"

"No, but let's guess Denver, shall we?"

"What's this Willie like?"

"Deadly," Delvecchio said. "Likes to hurt people, likes to kill. And he's got friends who like the same things."

"Why's he with . . . Ma?"

"Ma, Mother, Mother Baum, the Old Lady, she's called lots of things."

"Byrnes said she was called Queen of Fences."

Delvecchio smiled.

"That's her favorite. I think she may have coined it herself. Anyway, Willie's probably warmin' her bed for the same reason he does everythin' else— profit."

"So Willie probably went with the kids to Denver to . . . What? Teach them? Watch them? Help them?"

"You tell me. What'd you find out in Denver?"

Clint didn't bother telling Delvecchio that *he* hadn't found out anything, that he'd had to send Bat Masterson a telegram to try to find something out.

"A young man was seen in the company of the dead woman for a few days before her death."

"That would be Ben. Anybody see a young girl around?"

"Not that we know of."

"Yeah, but Ma would never send Ben alone. Bethany's the smart one."

"Yesterday Ma said Bethany was a stupid girl."

"That's because she hates her," Delvecchio said, "but Ma knows she needs her. Ben would be useless without Bethany."

"So what would happen if Bethany decided to leave Ma?"

"Well, Bethany's life would get better, Ben's would get worse, and Ma would probably hate the girl even more. In fact, I'd go so far as to say Bethany would make a bad enemy out of Ma."

"She came to see me."

"Bethany?"

Clint nodded. "Last night."

"What did she want?"

"She begged me not to kill Ben, told me he didn't kill the woman in Denver."

"She tell you who did?"

"Not a word. Either out of loyalty to Ma—"

"Or fear," Delvecchio finished. "Bethany's not afraid of Ma, but she'd be afraid of what Ma would do to Ben."

"The girl needs help," Clint said. "She needs somebody to advise her, help her make up her mind."

"Well, she's got somebody," Delvecchio said. "She'd just have to be smart enough to ask him."

"Who's that?"

"George Appo," the detective said. "Part Asian, part Irish, best pickpocket in the city."

"Did she learn it from him?"

Delvecchio nodded.

"George has two protégés, Bethany and a kid called Red."

"I've met him," Clint said. "I wasn't off the train ten seconds when I found his hand in my pocket."

"The kid's got a great touch," Delvecchio said. "I'm surprised and impressed you caught him."

"What about Bethany?"

"She's got talent, but she's not a natural like the kid."

"Anything romantic between her and Appo?"

"No," Delvecchio said. "He's only about ten years older than she is, but I don't think anything's goin' on between them. He's just her mentor."

"So then she'll go to him for help?"

"I'm sure if she goes to anybody it'll be him."

"Okay, good," Clint said, "then you take me to see him, and maybe we can get him to tell her what we want her to hear."

"What makes you think George Appo is gonna help you?" Delvecchio asked.

"He and I have a mutual friend who will vouch for me," Clint said.

"Sorry, friend," Delvecchio said, "but me and Appo are acquaintances, not friends."

"I wasn't talking about you," Clint said. "I was talking about Red."

"The kid? He might be hard to find."

"He told me to put the word out on the street and he'd hear about it."

"Okay," Delvecchio said. "I'll put the word out. Where should I say he can find you?"

"What's wrong with right here?"

Delvecchio looked down at his cup and said, "Well, for one, the coffee stinks."

THIRTY

Two hours and a lot of cups of weak coffee later, the kid Red came sauntering in.

"So, now you need Red's help, huh?" he asked, looking at Clint and Delvecchio. "Hey, I know you."

"Delvecchio."

"Right, the private detective. You put the word out that Mr. Adams wanted me, right?"

"Right."

Red looked at Clint.

"So what can I do for you, Mr. Gunsmith?"

"I want you to take me to see George Appo."

"George? Why?"

"Because I think a girl named Bethany needs help, and I think she's going to go to him for it."

"Whatsamatter with Bethany? Why don't she come to me for help? We're friends."

"Then all the more reason you should take me to see George," Clint said. "I want to help Bethany."

Red looked at Delvecchio.

"Is he tellin' me straight?"

"Yeah, kid," Delvecchio said. "He wants to help the girl."

"Well, okay," Red said. "I gotta talk to George first. Where will I find you?"

Clint looked down at his weak coffee.

"Right here."

"Right," Red said. "I'll be back in an hour."

As Red left, Clint suddenly slapped his forehead with his palm.

"What?" Delvecchio asked.

"I was supposed to be picked up this morning by Captain Byrnes."

"Oh, yeah. To go talk to those other fences. Well, now you don't have to do that."

"I know," Clint said, "but Byrnes doesn't know it."

"So he probably went without you," Delvecchio said. "It'll keep him busy."

"It'll probably make him mad."

"More coffee?"

"Do they serve beer here?"

"No."

Clint shrugged.

"I'll have some more weak coffee."

True to his word, Red was back in an hour.

"Okay," he said. "George says he'll talk to you."

"Not here, I hope," Clint said.

"No," Red said. "George has class. He wouldn't be caught dead in a place like this."

"Where then?"

"The Metropole."

"They have good coffee there," Delvecchio said.

"Okay," Clint said, standing up. "Let's go."

"Not the detective," Red said. "Just you."

"See?" Delvecchio said. "I told you. Not friends."

"I'll see you later," Clint said to the private detective.

"I'll come by your hotel."

"Lead on, little man," Clint said.

"Hey, my name's Red."

"Okay, Red," Clint said. "No offense meant."

The Metropole was indeed a classy place. Clint had been there once, years before, but it hadn't changed. He bet it still served the best steak in town.

"Come on," Red said. "George is inside already, at his table."

As they entered, they were stopped by a man in a tuxedo, but Red said, "Outta the way, we're here to see George."

"Oh, no," the man said, looking at Red, "it's you." He wrinkled his nose, as if he smelled something bad—and maybe he did.

"Yeah, I'm back." Red turned to Clint. "George is this way."

As he followed Red across the restaurant, Clint asked, "What's with you and the guy in the suit?"

"He don't think I'm clean enough to come to a joint like this," Red said. "But if George says it's okay, it's okay."

"George is a big man in this city, huh?"

"George is the biggest pickpocket in town," Red said, "the king."

Well, why not? Hadn't he already met the Queen of Fences?

Why not the King of Pickpockets?

THIRTY-ONE

As Clint and Red approached the table, a man stood up and extended his hand. His eyes were just slightly Asian, his hands slender, with tapered fingers. A pickpocket's perfect hands, Clint assumed. The man himself was not very tall, was slender and probably not yet thirty. He was dressed extremely well.

"Mr. Adams? I'm George Appo."

"Mr. Appo, it's a pleasure to meet you."

"Have a seat," Appo said. "Have you had lunch?"

"Actually, no," Clint said. "I've been drinking bad coffee for the past few hours."

"Well, we can fix that."

The two men sat down, and Appo waved a waiter over.

"A pot of coffee, Lee," Appo told the waiter. "Mind if I order for both of us?"

Clint said, "Be my guest."

"Steaks, Lee," Appo said. "With everything."

Lee, the young waiter, looked at Red and asked, "Three?"

"Two," Appo said. "Red, you better go."

"Aw, George . . ."

"Go ahead," Appo said. "Mr. Adams and I have to talk."

"Grown-up talk," Red said, nodding.

"That's right."

"Aw, gee . . ." Red said, but he turned and left with a desultory slouch to his shoulders.

"Red likes you, Mr. Adams," Appo said. "He doesn't usually take to strangers that quickly."

"I'm flattered."

"My point is, I wouldn't have agreed to see you unless Red vouched for you. Also, he said it had something to do with Bethany."

"It does. Have you seen her lately?"

"By lately you mean—"

"Today?"

"No. The last time I saw her was day before yesterday. It was right here, as a matter of fact. Has she gotten into trouble since then?"

"No," Clint said. "I think she got into trouble way before that—but let's not go that far back. Let's just go to Denver."

"She and Ben just got back from Denver."

"Where Ma sent them, right?"

"You'd have to ask Bethany."

"Look—" Clint said, stopping short when the waiter brought the coffeepot and two cups. He poured them full and then left.

"Taste it," Appo said.

Clint did.

"Good?"

"Very good," Clint said, "and miles better than what I've been drinking so far today."

"You were saying something about Denver?"

"A woman was killed and her house was cleaned out," Clint said. "I believe the goods are on their way here."

"To Ma, to be fenced?"

"That's what I think."

"Why does this put Bethany in trouble? She wouldn't kill anybody."

"What about Ben?"

"That boy? I'll tell you the truth, Bethany has the nerve to kill if she had to, but not that boy. He just doesn't have it in him."

"I don't think either one of them did it. I think it was a man named Willie O'Donnell."

"Well, that makes more sense," Appo said. "Willie's a born killer. He likes it."

"Bethany came to me and told me Ben didn't do it, but she wouldn't tell me who did. But she's got to tell somebody."

"Me?"

"You're her mentor, right?"

"Doesn't mean she'd put her head on the chopping block," Appo said. "If she told anyone, Ma would have Willie kill her."

"Really?"

"Ma Mandelbaum doesn't have it in her to love anybody but one person."

"Who's that? Willie O'Donnell?"

"No."

"Herself, then?"

"Wrong again. It's Ben."

"Ben? But she treats him—"

"Like dirt, I know," Appo said. "She's trying to toughen him up."

"And what about Bethany?"

"The truth?"

"I'd appreciate it."

"She's jealous of Bethany."

"Why?"

"Because she's smart," Appo said, "and because she doesn't need her."

The waiter returned with steaming plates of steak, potatoes, and other vegetables. Both men leaned back so he could put them down.

"She needs help, Mr. Appo," Clint said, "and I'm willing to help her."

"What does she have to do?"

"Tell you or me who killed the woman in Denver," Clint said. "I'll make sure he can't hurt her."

"And what about Ma?"

"If Willie goes away for killing Mrs. Wellington, I bet he'll take Ma with him."

"He just might," Appo said. "So you want me to get her to talk?"

"I want you to give her somebody to talk to. A friendly ear, some friendly advice, whatever it takes."

Appo picked up his knife and fork, used the knife to point to Clint's plate.

"Why don't we eat our lunch," he said, "and while we're doing that I'll think over your proposition."

Clint picked up his own utensils and looked down at his plate.

"That's a proposition I can agree to right now," he said.

THIRTY-TWO

The meal was the best Clint had had in a while. The waiter brought a second pot of coffee.

"Dessert?" Appo asked.

"You usually have dessert after lunch?"

"Lunch, supper, there's always room for dessert," the pickpocket said.

"Not for me," Clint said. "Thanks."

"Okay, Lee, not today," Appo said.

"Yes, sir."

As the waiter walked away, Clint said, "So what do you say, George? You want to help save your girl's life?"

"You think it'll come to that?" Appo asked.

"Do you think she'll try to leave Ma eventually?" Clint asked.

"I've thought so for a long time," Appo said. "The only thing holding her back is Ben."

"What if she tried to take Ben with her?"

"Ma would kill 'er."

"And if she gave Willie up?" Clint asked.

"Ma would kill 'er."

"And if she tried to leave Ma on her own, even without Ben?"

"Okay, I get you," Appo said. "No matter which way she goes, she's going to end up dead."

"Unless we help her."

"Okay," Appo said. "I'll talk to her, but without you around. I don't want you pressuring the girl."

"That's fine with me, George. I want two things— the killer and to help Bethany."

"Why would one of those things be as important to you as the other? You don't know the girl."

"She came to me to plead for her brother," Clint said. "I think she's loyal, and brave. And I met Ma Mandelbaum. I'd like to get Bethany away from her."

"What about Ben?"

"Him, too."

"Do you want to rescue them from a life of crime?" Appo asked. "It's been pretty good to me."

"No," Clint said. "Not from a life of crime. Just from death."

On the steps outside the Metropole, Appo said, "I'll get word to you after I've talked to her."

"Which way do you think she'll go?"

"I don't know," Appo said. "Maybe to New Jersey. She's got a mind of her own."

"I hope you can convince her," Clint said. "I'll wait to hear from you."

Clint started down the steps, Appo remaining at the top, watching him.

"Mr. Adams."

At the bottom Clint turned and looked up.

"I want to thank you in advance."

"For what?"

"For trying to help."

"Trying," Clint said, "takes so little effort, I wonder why more people don't do it."

"Many try," Appo said. "Few actually do."

"Given the opportunity," Clint said, "I can and will do a lot more than try."

Appo nodded. "You just might get the opportunity, my new friend," he said.

THIRTY-THREE

When Clint got back to his hotel, there was a uniformed policeman waiting for him in the lobby.

"Captain Byrnes would like to see you, sir," the man said. "He sent me to fetch you."

"What's your name?"

"Edwards, sir."

"Well, Officer Edwards," Clint said, "let's go. We don't want to keep the captain waiting."

Edwards drove Clint to Mulberry Street in a buggy and dropped him out front.

"He's waiting for you, sir," Edwards said. "I have to take care of the horse."

"Thanks for the ride, Officer."

Clint went inside, prepared to face an angry Captain Thomas Byrnes.

The front desk sergeant decided to walk him back to Byrnes's office himself. Maybe he wanted to see Clint's head get bitten off. But when Clint entered Byrnes's office, the man barely looked at him, and said to the sergeant, "Close the door."

"Yes, sir."

"Captain," Clint said, "I'm really sorry. I got called away and wasn't able to contact you in time to keep you from coming to pick me up this morning."

"Contacted by who, I wonder?" Byrnes asked. "Delvecchio, or George Appo?"

"Appo?"

"I have eyes and ears all over this city, Mr. Adams," Byrnes said. "I know who had breakfast with Delvecchio and lunch with Appo. What's going on?"

"I'm doing what Talbot Roper asked me to do, Captain," Clint said. "Trying to find out who killed Libby Wellington. I figure to talk to anyone I can talk to who might help me."

"What kind of help do you think you can get from George Appo?"

"I don't know," Clint said. "Somebody told me he knew things about Ma Mandelbaum."

"Ma Mandelbaum," Byrnes said. "I see you learned more of her nicknames."

"Yes."

"From who? Mr. Delvecchio or Mr. Appo?"

"Does it matter?"

"No, actually, it doesn't," Byrnes said. "What does matter is I've made myself available to you for help and you seem to prefer the help of criminals."

"Delvecchio's not—"

"He might as well be," the captain said, cutting him off. "I'd like to know why you felt the need to go to George Appo."

"Okay," Clint said. "I'll tell you the truth."

"Please."

"The girl came to me last night."

"What girl?"

"Bethany."

"What did she want?"

"She wanted to plead for the life of her brother, Ben," Clint said.

"For his life?"

"She had it in her head that I came here from Denver to kill him."

"I have to admit I had the same thought."

"That I wanted to kill Ben?"

"No, that you wanted to kill whoever the killer turns out to be," Byrnes said. "After all, your reputation—"

"I'm sure an experienced lawman like you doesn't believe everything he hears, Captain."

"No, of course not," Byrnes said. "Go on. What else did she say?"

"She told me that Ben didn't kill the woman in Denver."

"Did she say who did?"

"No, she wouldn't say that."

"Why not?"

"I suspect she didn't want it traced back to Ma."

"And what conclusion did you draw from all this?"

"Several, as a matter of fact," Clint said. "First, that Ma is the fence involved. Second, that she sent her man Willie to Denver with those kids, and he probably killed the Wellington woman."

"And is there a third?"

"Yes," Clint said. "I decided that the girl needs help."

"So you went to George Appo?"

"I, uh, heard somewhere that he's her mentor."

"If you mean he's trying to make her into as big a criminal as he is, you're right."

"Captain," Clint said, "I want to keep that girl alive. That's all."

"And catch a killer."

"Yes."

"And you think you can do these things without me?" Byrnes asked.

Clint wondered if all he was dealing with here was a wounded ego. He hoped so. He wanted Byrnes to be a bigger man than that, if only because Tal Roper recommended him so highly.

"No, Captain, I don't," he said carefully. "I'm trying to use every tool I can find."

"Well," Byrnes said, "you seem to have isolated Fredericka Mandelbaum as the fence involved. And I concur that puts Willie O'Donnell in the picture. Bethany could kill, but I don't think she did, and as for Ben—well, he hasn't got the backbone to kill."

Maybe he had too much sense, or too gentle a nature, Clint thought. He wouldn't hold either one of those things against the young man.

"Did you talk to those other fences?"

"I did," Byrnes said. "I thought either of them would be good for this, but as I said, you seem to have pinpointed Ma for us."

"So what's next?"

"I'll have her watched," Byrnes said. "We'll know when Willie O'Donnell gets back to town, and then we'll have another conversation with both Ma and him."

"Sounds good to me."

"That doesn't seem to leave you much to do until that

happens," Byrnes said. "Oh, wait, you're trying to save Bethany's immortal soul. I guess you can continue to work on that."

Clint stood up and said, "I think I'll do just that, Captain," and walked out.

THIRTY-FOUR

When Clint left police headquarters, he felt kind of bad. Talbot Roper had sent him to Byrnes because the two men were friends, and maybe Clint'd disrespected the man. On the other hand, Roper had asked him for a favor, and he'd agreed to try to do the job. If dealing with Delvecchio and Appo got the job done, then that was what he was going to do.

He walked up Mulberry Street and managed to wave down a passing cab. He told the driver to take him to the Belvedere Hotel.

He had little to do now but wait to hear from somebody—Delvecchio, Byrnes, or George Appo, after he'd talked with Bethany. When the cab left him off, instead of going into the hotel he went next door, into the tavern. The lunch he'd had with Appo was still sitting heavily on his stomach, but he felt the need for a cold beer. He easily found a place at the bar and ordered one.

"Angie ain't in yet," the bartender said.

"What?"

"Angie," the man said. "She ain't in yet. She'll be in later."

"Oh, okay," Clint said. "Thanks."

The man nodded, went to get the beer.

George Appo used Red to find Bethany and get her to
meet him at his place. When she arrived, she was very
agitated.

"I was lookin' for you all last night," she said. "You
weren't home, you weren't at the Metropole."

"I was out working until late," he said. "I didn't
know you were looking for me—but I'm looking for
you."

"What's wrong?"

"I should ask you the same thing. Why were you
looking for me?"

She wrung her hands and sat down.

"I want to get out, George."

"Out?"

"Away from Ma."

"Well . . ."

"What's that mean?"

"It's a coincidence, that's all."

"What do you mean?"

"I had a meeting with Clint Adams."

"Why did you want to see him?"

"I didn't," Appo said. "He wanted to see me. Something about you asking him not to kill Ben."

"I can't protect Ben anymore," she said, shaking her
head. "I have to watch out for myself from now on."

"Well, that's music to my ears," Appo said, "and,
I'll bet, to Clint Adams's ears, too."

"Why?"

"He claims he wants to help you get away from Ma
without getting killed."

"Oh sure," she said. "All I have to do is tell him who killed that woman in Denver."

"So tell him."

"And get killed, anyway?"

"Adams says he won't let that happen."

"And how's he gonna do that?"

"Well . . . he is the Gunsmith."

"This is not the old West, George," she said. "Willie O'Donnell is not gonna stand in the street with a six-shooter."

"I think Adams can handle himself, Bethany," Appo said.

She looked at him, frowning. "You think I should tell him that Willie killed that woman?"

"He did, didn't he?"

"Yes."

"Are you positive?"

"Ben saw him."

"Ben actually saw him kill her?"

"Yes."

George walked around the room, rubbing his chin.

"Ben told you he saw Willie kill the woman?"

"Yes."

"Then why isn't Ben dead?"

"What?"

"If he's a witness to Willie killing somebody, Willie would kill him."

"Don't forget, Ben is Ma's son," Bethany said. "Willie wouldn't kill him."

"He would if he could keep Ma from finding out it was him."

Bethany shook her head.

"I can't worry about Ben anymore," she said. "Not after . . ."

"Not after what?"

"Never mind," she said. "All right, I'll talk to him if you say so, George."

"I'll set it up. Where do you want to do it?"

"I don't care," she said, hanging her head.

"Look, honey," Appo said, "you stay here until I come for you. I'll set it up at the Metropole."

"Okay," she said.

"Get some rest. I'll be back as soon as I get word to Adams."

"George . . ."

Appo patted her shoulder. "You're doing the right thing, Bethany."

"I hope so."

THIRTY-FIVE

"She said what?"

Ben had decided the night before not to tell Ma about Bethany until morning. After that he found a saloon and drank until he staggered home and fell asleep on the floor. Now this morning, with a raging headache, he was giving her the news.

"She said she's not comin' back, Ma."

He flinched, thinking she was going to slap him, but she didn't. It surprised him. The look on her face also surprised him. He'd never seen it before, and couldn't identify it.

"What'd she say, exactly?" Ma asked.

"She said she ain't comin' back."

"Ever?"

"That's right, Ma."

"And did she ask you to go with her?"

"Well . . . yeah."

"Why didn't you?"

"I couldn't leave you, Ma."

"You couldn't, huh?" she asked.

She turned and walked away from him, folding her arms with her head down.

"Ma?"

She turned and glared at him.

"You get her back."

"What?"

"You heard me," Ma said tightly. "Bring her back here."

"But, Ma, she don't wanna come back. She don't wanna come back, ever."

"I don't care," Ma said. "I want her back."

"But . . . why?" Ben was puzzled. "Ma, I thought you hated Bethany."

"Oh, don't be a fool all your life, Ben."

"You mean you don't hate her?"

"I mean I need her."

"What for? You got me."

"I need her to take over this business when I'm gone."

"But Ma . . . I thought I—"

"Oh, you *are* gonna be a fool all your life, aren't you, Ben? Just like your father."

"My father?"

"He was a fool, always wanting me to play it straight. Well, look what playing it straight got him. Dead at an early age."

"What's that got to do with Bethany?"

"That girl has somethin' your father didn't have and you don't have, either."

"What's that?"

"Smarts."

"But you always said she was stupid."

"She is, about a lot of things," Ma said. "But she's got a brain, and I intend to use that brain."

"By treatin' her bad? By always callin' her stupid? How's that usin' her brain?"

"Look," Ma said, pointing her finger in his face, "you just go and get that sister of yours back here. Nobody walks out on Ma."

"Ma, why don't you—"

"Look, Benny boy," she said. "If you don't bring her back, I'll just send Willie to get her when he gets back."

"Willie would kill her."

"No, he won't," she said. "Not if he wants to stay with me."

"He just wants your money, Ma."

Now she did slap him.

"You don't know anything about Willie."

"I know he's always tryin' to touch Bethany. I know that."

"That's a lie."

"I know he killed that woman in Denver," he went on. "I saw him."

"I told you I'd talk to him about that when he got back."

"What's to talk about? He killed her. He's a murderer. Sooner or later he's gonna get in big trouble, and take you down with him."

"Stop talkin', Ben," she warned. "Just stop talkin' and go get that no-good sister of yours back here. You hear me, boy?"

He stared at her, but her eyes were so hard and menacing he had to look away. He knew his father had

had the same problem. He could never look her in the eye and stand up to her.

"Okay, Ma," he said finally. "Okay. I'll go and get her."

"And, Benny?"

"Yeah, Ma?"

She put her hands on her hips and fixed him with that stare again.

"Don't come back here without her."

After Ben left, Fredericka Mandelbaum paced the floor, rubbing her hands together. She'd been trying to toughen Ben up for years, but knew that it wasn't going to work. The only chance she had to leave something behind was Bethany. She hated the girl because she was a constant reminder of her father, but she had to admit that the girl had smarts. She was a talented pickpocket and, given time, would learn the business and become the best fence in Manhattan—better, even, than Ma.

Fredericka simply could not allow Bethany to walk away. It had to be George Appo who'd been filling her head with this nonsense about not coming back, and perhaps the arrival of this Clint Adams from the West. She didn't know for sure about Adams, but she did know that the man was here from Denver looking for whoever had killed that woman.

She had no doubt that it was Willie who had killed her, but the cow probably had it coming. When Willie got back, he and his boys would take care of the Gunsmith.

But the Queen of Fences could not wait for Willie to take care of the King of Pickpockets. She was going to have to get it done herself.

THIRTY-SIX

Once again Appo used Red to get a message to Clint Adams.

"I'm gettin' real tired of bein' used as a messenger boy," Red said, "and then bein' sent away when the talkin' starts."

"If you do this," Appo said, "Bethany will know that you helped her."

"I'd do anythin' for Bethany, George," Red said.

So he went to Clint's hotel and found him waiting in his room to hear from . . . somebody.

"George wants you to meet him and Bethany at the Metropole," Red told him when Clint opened his door.

"When?"

"Noon."

"You gonna be there?" Clint asked.

"Naw," Red said. "I don't wanna hear a bunch of grown-up talk."

Clint smiled. It was better for Red to sound like he was skipping the meeting of his own accord.

"Okay," Clint said. "Tell them I'll be there."

He closed the door, thinking this was the break he

needed. If Bethany told him that Willie did the murder, then it was just a matter of days before O'Donnell got back to town, and Clint would have him.

Ma had sent word out for Bull Benson, and when the front door to her shop opened, she thought it was him. She was surprised to see that it was Willie O'Donnell.

"How's my girl?" Willie called out.

Ma stared at him.

"Whataya doin' back so soon?"

"Is that any way to greet yer everlovin' man, lass?" he asked.

Ma let the Irishman take her in his arms and give her a big hug, then she pushed him away and slapped his hands down.

"Where's the merchandise?"

"Still on the way with the boys," Willie said. "I hopped a train to get home to you sooner."

"Well, for a change you did the right thing," she said. "Things have gone to hell here."

"And you need ol' Willie to fix it all, right?"

"Ol' Willie needs to shut up and listen."

So he did.

Clint went up the steps of the Metropole and inside. The same man in a tuxedo greeted him.

"Can I help you, sir?"

"I'm here to see George Appo."

The man looked behind him.

"No kid today," Clint said. "Just me."

The man looked relieved.

"This way, sir."

He followed the man to the same table as last time,

where this time George Appo was sitting with a nervous-looking Bethany.

Appo stood, and he and Clint shook hands.

"Coffee," Clint said to the waiter who appeared at his elbow.

He sat across from Bethany, to Appo's right.

"Hello, Bethany."

"I'm only here because George said I should talk to you."

"But you want to talk to me, Bethany," Clint said. "Or you wouldn't have come to see me at my hotel."

"That was for Ben," she said. "I ain't doin' that no more. From now on I'm lookin' out for me."

"Does that mean you're leaving Ma?"

"Yeah."

"She's not going to like that."

"I don't care."

"Do you think she'll come after you?"

She hesitated, then said, "Probably."

"And who will she send?"

Bethany sighed. "She'll send Ben first to try to talk me into comin' back, and if I don't, then she'll send Willie."

"And you're afraid of Willie, right?"

"No, I ain't afraid of Willie," she said, "but I ain't stupid. I see what you're gettin' at. Willie's likely to kill me if I don't go back."

"Tell me something else."

"What?"

"Why will Ma want you back?"

"Because nobody leaves Ma."

"She says you're stupid," Clint said. "Do you think she believes that?"

"No," Bethany said. "She hates me, but she doesn't think I'm stupid. Not really."

"So she wants you back because you're smart."

"It don't matter why she wants me back," Bethany said. "I ain't goin'."

"Well, we can keep Willie from coming after you," Clint said.

"Yeah?"

"All you have to do is tell me who killed Libby Wellington in Denver."

Bethany looked at Appo, who nodded.

"It was Willie."

"Why'd he kill her?"

"She and Ben got back too early."

"And how do you know Willie killed her?"

"Ben told me."

"He saw him do it?"

"Yeah, through a window he saw Willie hit her over the head,"

"With what?"

"I don't know," she said. "What does that matter? Willie's your killer. Now you'll kill him, right?"

"Not exactly," Clint said, "but I'll see that he pays for killing her."

"Fine," she said, "whatever you want to do."

"You should move out of wherever you're living now," Clint said. He looked at Appo. "Can we put her someplace safe?"

"I got a place."

"Okay," Clint said. "Bethany, why don't you wait for us by the front door? I got something I want to talk to George about."

She shrugged, stood up, then said, "Now I know how Red feels."

She left the table and went to the front.

"What's on your mind?"

"Is Willie O'Donnell stupid?"

"He's not stupid," Appo said, "but he's not intelligent. He's . . . crafty."

"If Ben saw him kill the woman, why would he leave him alive?"

"I don't know. Maybe because he's Ma Baum's son."

"That's what Bethany told me when I asked, but I didn't buy it."

"So what are you thinking?"

"I'm just asking questions."

George called the waiter over, paid the bill, and then he and Clint joined Bethany at the door.

"I'll go with Bethany to her place to get her things and then take her to my place. She can stay there until I get her another place."

Clint nodded, and the three of them went out the door. They were halfway down the stairs when the shots started. Clint heard them, then pushed Bethany to the side and hit the ground. He rolled down the steps the rest of the way, banging his left elbow painfully, but producing his gun with his right hand.

He came up on one knee, looking for the shooter or shooters, but they were gone. One barrage was all they had the nerve for.

He looked up the stairs at Appo, who seemed to be in shock. His face was white as a sheet.

"You okay?" Clint asked.

"I think so." Appo patted his body. "I'm—I'm not shot."

"Where's Beth—" Clint said, looking around and stopping short when he spotted her lying on the steps facedown.

"Bethany?" he called, thinking she was too scared to lift her head, but she didn't move.

"Oh God," Appo said. They both rushed to her and saw the little rivulet of blood that was rolling from beneath her body.

THIRTY-SEVEN

Bethany was taken to Bellevue Hospital with two bullets in her, one in the chest and another in the shoulder. Clint had gotten to her first and done what he could to stanch the bleeding until help could arrive. It was a miracle that she was still alive.

In the waiting room of Bellevue, Clint asked Appo, "Did you see the shooters?"

"Shooters?"

"Sounded like more than one to me."

"Oh, no, I—I didn't see. I have to admit I was . . . cowering."

"That's a good thing to do when somebody's shooting at you, especially if you're unarmed."

"I feel like a coward," Appo said. "I did nothing. At least you pushed Bethany to the side."

"Big deal," Clint said. "I might have pushed her right into the path of those bullets."

"I saw you," Appo said. "You tried to protect her, and at the same time you drew your gun. You were ready."

"Drawing my gun is a reflex," Clint said.

"I guess you really are the Gunsmith," Appo said. "I mean, the man they say you are."

"You can never tell."

A doctor came toward them and they both turned to face him.

"I don't know how, but she's still alive. We'll know more if she lasts another twenty-four hours." He was an older man, in his fifties, with gray hair. He shook his head. "Who'd want to shoot down a young girl like that?"

As he walked away, Clint said, "I think we know who those shots were meant for."

"Yeah," Appo said. "Me."

"I was thinking me."

"No," Appo said. "Ma probably got word that I was helping Bethany, and she tried to have me killed."

"By who?"

"If Willie was in town, I'd say him and one of his boys. If not, then just somebody Ma keeps around to do her dirty work—somebody like Bull Benson, maybe."

"Where do I find Bull Benson?"

"Hey, we don't know that he did it."

"If he didn't, maybe he knows who did."

"You'll find him someplace in Five Points," Appo said. "But you can't go there alone."

"I don't intend to."

"I don't have a gun, but—"

"You stay here in case Bethany wakes up," Clint said. "She'll need to know somebody's here. I have a man in mind to take with me."

"Okay, but— Uh-oh, here comes Byrnes."

Clint turned and saw Captain Byrnes storming toward him, his face so suffused with blood it seemed to be glowing. Trailing behind him were two uniformed police officers.

"You turned the street in front of the Metropole into the old West?" he demanded. "What were you thinking?"

"Here," Clint said, holding his gun out to Byrnes.

"What's that for?"

"Check it," Clint said. "I never fired a shot."

Byrnes hesitated, then took the gun, sniffed it, and then handed it back.

"What happened?"

"Somebody just opened fire on us."

"Who's 'us'?" Byrnes asked. He still hadn't looked at George Appo.

"Appo, Bethany, and me."

"Anybody hit?"

"Bethany," Clint said. "She took two bullets, one in the chest and one in the shoulder."

"Is she dead?"

"No."

"That's too bad," Byrnes said, then added, "I mean, too bad she was shot."

"She was almost certainly not the target," Clint said.

"You?"

"That's what I say, but Appo thinks it was him."

"Why?"

"He thinks Ma doesn't like that he's helping Bethany leave her."

"She left Ma?"

"That's right."

"Then she may well have been the target."

Clint shook his head. "I don't think even Ma Mandelbaum would do that."

"You're thinking there's something inside of that woman, some semblance of . . . maternal instinct?"

"That's what I'm thinking," Clint said.

"I can't go along with that thinking," Byrnes said. "I'm going to have to go and have a talk with Ma."

He didn't invite Clint along, and Clint didn't ask. He had his own plans.

"Appo, don't make any plans to leave the city," Byrnes said.

"Captain," Appo said very calmly, "I never leave the city."

Byrnes just nodded, then turned and waved to his men to follow him.

"If he goes and talks to Ma," Clint said, "she might come here."

"You think she will?"

"I don't know," Clint said. "You and Byrnes know her better than I do. Is she that cold that she'd try to have Bethany killed?"

"I still think either me or you was the intended victim," Appo said. "It makes more sense."

"Well, just don't be surprised if she shows up here," Clint said. "Meanwhile, I'm going to go and find Bull Benson."

"You sure you've got somebody—"

"I've got a good man to go with me," Clint said, "and he's local."

"Be careful in Five Points," Appo said. "They don't like strangers there."

"I've been to a lot of places where they didn't like strangers," Clint said.

THIRTY-EIGHT

Charles Dickens had this to say about Five Points:

"This is the place: these narrow ways diverging to the right and left, and reeking every where with dirt and filth. . . . See how the rotten beams are tumbling down, and how the patched and broken windows seem to scowl dimly, like eyes that have been hurt in drunken frays. Many of these pigs live here. Do they ever wonder why their masters walk upright in lieu of going on all-fours? and why they talk instead of grunting?"

Five Points was also known as the Sixth Ward, but the name came from the five converging streets of Mulberry, Anthony, Cross, Orange, and Little Water streets.

Clint met with Delvecchio and told him where he wanted to go.

"Five Points."

"That's right," Clint said. "Seems that's where I'll find somebody named Bull Benson."

"I know Benson."

"Do you know everybody in this town who walks on the wrong side of the law?"

Delvecchio thought a moment, then said, "Yeah, pretty much. Ain't that the kind of person you need right now?"

"I guess it is."

"I'll bet you know a lot of men in the West who walk on the wrong side."

Clint thought a moment, then said, "Yeah, I do."

"Okay," Delvecchio said, "Five Points it is."

The cab they took would not take them into Five Points.

"I ain't that crazy, gents," the driver said.

"That's okay," Delvecchio said. "We'll walk from here."

They got out and Clint saw that they were on Little Water Street. They walked two or three blocks and Clint suddenly noticed the difference. The buildings were more run-down, and the decay became apparent not only to the eye but to the nose as well.

"Where are we going?"

"We won't have to try very hard to find Benson," Delvecchio said. "If I'm right, he'll be in this Irish saloon I know of."

"That'll be handy," Clint said. "I could use a beer right about how."

"Um, are you carrying that little gun of yours?" Delvecchio asked.

Clint reached behind his back, inside his jacket, and came out with his modified Colt.

"No," he said. "I thought my regular sidearm might come in handy if someone tried to shoot at me from across the street again."

"I feel better already," Delvecchio said as Clint tucked the gun away.

Bull Benson was standing at the bar enjoying his beer and his audience. He was regaling them with tales of old fights and conquests, stories they'd all heard before but were afraid to mention. He was a huge man, six foot six, and very wide. No one in Five Points had ever seen him bested in a fight.

When the bar suddenly grew quiet, he looked toward the door and saw the two men standing just inside.

"Is that Delvecchio?" he called across the floor. "Who's your friend, Delvecchio?"

"Hello, Bull," Delvecchio said. "Can we have a word?"

Benson spread his arms—a huge wingspan—and said, "I don't have any secrets from my friends."

"We're lookin' for your friend Willie O'Donnell," Delvecchio said.

"Get away from me!" Benson growled at the men around him. Then he waved to Delvecchio and Clint. "Come 'ere."

"Don't be askin' for Willie out loud like that," Benson told Delvecchio. "Who's your friend?"

"His name is Clint Adams. He's lookin' for Willie."

"Why?"

"Somebody took a shot at me today," Clint said. "I think it was Willie."

"Willie's out of town."

"Then a friend of Willie's."

"I'm the only friend Willie's got," Benson said, "and I didn't take a shot at you. If I was gonna kill ya, I'd do it with my hands."

"I can believe it."

"Are you law?"

"Do I look like law?"

"You look like somethin'," Benson said. "Somethin' I don't like."

"Bull, you still workin' for Ma Baum?"

"I ain't never worked for her."

"You work for Willie, and Willie works for her," Delvecchio said.

Benson laughed and said, "Yeah, right. Willie works for her."

"What do you mean by that?" Clint asked.

"You ain't the law," Benson said. "I don't hafta talk ta you."

"Bull—" Delvecchio said.

"Get out, Del," Benson said. "I ain't gotta talk ta either one of you."

"Get a message to your pal Willie," Clint said. "I know what he did, and I'm going to make him pay—unless he stops me."

"With talk like that, friend, he will."

"I'd like to see him try."

Benson turned to face Clint head-on, looking down at him.

"I'll give him the message, friend," Benson said. "And you know what? I hope he sends me."

Clint smiled up at Bull Benson and said, "You better hope he doesn't."

After Clint and Delvecchio left, Bull Benson had another beer. When his audience tried to come back, he waved his arms and said, "Stay away!"

He knew Willie was back in town. He also knew

that Ben and Willie had tried to kill George Appo and Clint Adams earlier that day. But how did Adams know that?

Benson finished his beer and went out the back door.

Outside Delvecchio said, "Why'd you do that?"

"Do what?"

"You practically called him out," the detective said. "Willie, too."

"Not practically. I did call them out."

"You got a death wish?"

"No," Clint said. "This is just the way I do things."

"In the West, maybe," Delvecchio said. "This ain't very subtle, Clint."

"They'll find out where I'm staying, and they'll come for me," Clint told him. "This time I'll be ready for them."

"Well, then," Delvecchio said, "so will I."

THIRTY-NINE

George Appo looked up when he heard the commotion. Ma Mandelbaum was stalking down the hall toward him with Ben trailing behind her.

"What the hell happened?" she demanded of Appo.

"You tell me, Ma."

"Whataya mean?"

"You sent somebody after me," he said, "or after Adams. Or maybe both of us. They got Bethany instead."

"Whataya talkin' about?" Ma asked. "Is she dead?"

"No," Appo said, "and by some miracle she's holding on."

"What the hell—where did this happen?"

"On the steps of the Metropole."

"And where's Adams?"

"He went looking for your boys."

"What boys?"

"Willie, or Bull Benson. Maybe both."

"Willie shot Bethany?"

"I don't know, Ma," Appo said. "Who'd you send? Whoever it was, they shot Bethany."

"I'll kill that sonofabitch!" she said, teeth clenched.

"Who?" Appo asked. "Who did you send?"

"Never mind," Ma said. "Never you mind." She turned to Ben. "Find Willie, and tell him I want him here—now!"

"Yes, Ma."

"You can go now," she told Appo.

"No, I think I'll stay," he said. "When she comes to, she's going to want to see a friendly face, don't you think?"

Ben knew exactly where Willie was—in a small saloon down on the Bowery.

"Ma wants you at the hospital," he said, finding Willie at the bar.

"She does, huh?"

"She's mad."

"She'll be even madder after I get through talkin' to her, won't she, Benny boy?"

"Willie—"

Willie waved and Bull Benson came over, towering over Ben.

"Benny boy, you and Bull are goin' over ta Clint Adams's hotel."

"What for?"

"You're gonna kill him."

"Me? But I—"

"Who was with Ma at the hospital?"

"G-George is there."

"Appo," Willie said. "Ah, that's good. So I'll go to the hospital and take care of George, and you boys take care of Adams."

"But I can't—" Ben said.

"I know, kid," Willie said, "that's exactly why you'll be able to. He'll never see it comin'."

Willie took out a gun and handed it to Ben.

"We goin' to your room?" Delvecchio asked as they reached the Belvedere Hotel.

"No," Clint said. "I thought we might as well wait in the tavern, have a beer."

They entered the tavern and found two places at the bar.

"You think they'll come today?"

"The sooner the better."

"What if they just stay outside and wait for us to come out?"

"If somebody called you out, what would you do?"

"I'd come in and get it over with, but these men—"

"Ego," Clint said. "They'll want to get it over with, too."

"You're talkin' about Western ego," Delvecchio said. "Willie O'Donnell is a wolf. He's cunning. He's not ruled by ego."

"So what will he do?"

"He'll try to do something you won't expect."

"Like what?"

"He'll come up with somethin'," Delvecchio said. "I'm just sayin' be careful."

"You know," Clint said, "it would have been very easy for O'Donnell to separate himself from his men and the merchandise and come back early."

"I'm surprised by one thing."

"What's that?"

"Willie's good at killin'," Delvecchio said. "What happened on the steps of the Metropole was sloppy."

"Maybe he rushed it."

"Yeah," Delvecchio said, "maybe. Still surprises me, though."

FORTY

"Not the hotel," Bull Benson said to Ben.

"What?"

Benson pointed next door.

"They'll be in the tavern."

"But—"

"Come on, boy," Benson said. "A man needs a drink while he's waitin' ta die."

Benson grabbed Ben's arm and pulled him over to the tavern.

"You go inside, you walk up to Adams, you talk to him for a minute, and then you pull the gun and shoot him right in the belly. You got it?"

"I guess . . ."

"This ain't the first time you pulled a trigger, ya know."

Ben blanched, then nodded, buttoning his jacket as he went inside.

"What'd you say about something unexpected?" Clint asked.

Delvecchio looked at the door and saw Ben enter with his jacket buttoned.

"Oh, no . . ."

"Go out the back and around," Clint said. "I'll take care of Ben."

"Great," Delvecchio said. "I can just imagine who's waitin' outside."

He headed for the rear door as Ben made his way to the bar.

The gun felt heavy in Ben's belt and he had the feeling that everybody in the tavern was looking at him, and could see the gun clearly. His heart was pounding because he thought he was going to die today.

And he deserved it.

Clint moved his beer mug so that it was sitting near his left hand. His right hand was hanging at his side where it would have been if he'd been wearing a holster.

When Ben reached the bar, he said, "Hello, Mr. Adams."

"Ben. I thought you'd be at the hospital."

"Ma sent me away."

"To do what?"

"Huh?"

"What does she want you to do, Ben?" Clint asked.

"She, uh, wanted me to find Willie."

"Is she mad at Willie? For shooting Bethany?"

Ben's eyes slid away. Clint saw his hand move to unbutton his jacket.

"Mr. Adams," he said, "I done somethin' real bad."

"What's that, Ben?" Clint was wondering if Ben was going to confess to killing Libby Wellington in Denver. Had they been after the wrong man all this time?

"I—I let Willie, uh, talk me into . . ."

"Talk you into what, Ben?" Clint asked. "Come on, how bad can it be?"

"Oh, it's bad."

"Ben, did you kill that woman in Denver?"

"No!" Ben said. "I didn't, I swear. It was Willie."

"Then what did you do?"

"I— It was me . . . shootin' at you in front of the Metropole."

"What?" That wasn't what Clint was expecting to hear. "Why? Wait . . . I heard two shooters."

"Yeah, it was me and Willie. Mr. Adams, I may have shot Bethany."

"Ben . . ."

"And now," Ben said, putting his hand to his belt, "I'm supposed to shoot you." He took the gun out, then laid it on the bar. "But I can't."

Clint, who had tensed when the boy touched his gun, relaxed. He picked up the gun and tucked it into his own belt. The boy had hung his head and tears were streaming down his face.

"It's okay, Ben," Clint said, patting the boy on the shoulder. "Where's Willie now?"

"He went to the hospital."

"For what?"

"He said I was supposed to kill you, and he was gonna go kill George Appo."

Clint grabbed Ben's arm and said, "Come on," and dragged him to the door.

When they got outside, Delvecchio was standing over Bull Benson, who was out cold on the ground.

"What happened?" Clint asked.

"I hit him from behind," Delvecchio said. "I told you, no ego here. You gotta be crafty."

Appo saw Willie O'Donnell before Ma Mandelbaum did. From the look on Willie's face, Appo wished he'd carried a gun.

Ma saw the look on Appo's face and turned.

"Did you do this?" she demanded as Willie O'Donnell reached her. "Did you shoot Bethany?"

"That little bitch?" Willie asked. "You never had anythin' good to say abut her, and now yer yellin' at me, askin' if I shot 'er?"

"You were supposed to kill Clint Adams, or him," Ma said, pointing a finger at Appo. "Not Bethany."

"What the hell is the difference, Ma?" Willie shouted. "Adams is bein' taken care of, and I'll do Appo right now."

With that, Willie pulled a gun from his belt and pointed it at Appo.

"Hold it, O'Donnell!" Clint shouted from down the hall.

Willie turned, saw Clint, and brought his gun around. Clint's gun was in his hand, and as he fired from down the hall he thought he heard another shot.

Willie staggered, his gun fell from his hand, and he collapsed to the floor, dead. Clint walked up to the body to examine it and saw that Willie had been shot in the chest—and in the back. He looked at Ma, saw her tucking a small gun away into the folds of her dress.

"Even if I did want that stupid girl dead," she muttered, "I'd do it myself."

FORTY-ONE

Clint looked around Grand Central Station terminal, then suddenly felt a hand in his pocket.

"That you, Red?"

"Ha, I was deliberately sloppy that time," Red said with a smile. "Are you really leavin'?"

Clint looked down at the dirty-faced little urchin and said, "Yes, I'm really leaving."

"Aren't you glad Bethany is gonna be all right?" Red asked.

"I sure am, Red," Clint said.

It had been touch-and-go for a while, but after three days the doctors were able to say that she would live. Clint did not have the time to stay and see how the whole Ma-Ben-Bethany relationship turned out. He hoped that Bethany would go through with her decision to leave Ma Mandelbaum, but he wasn't sure that going with George Appo was the best decision, either.

"If you ever come back, look me up, huh?" Red said. "I'll be older then."

"Yes," Clint said, "so will I, Red."

Red spotted Captain Byrnes coming their way and

said, "I gotta go. Bye, Clint. We're friends now, right? I'm friends with the Gunsmith?"

"That's right, Red," Clint said. "We're friends."

Red disappeared in the crowd, no doubt putting the touch on as many of them as he could.

"Mr. Adams," Byrnes said, "I'm glad I caught you."

"Captain."

They shook hands. They had not become friends, as Clint and Red had.

"I thought you'd like to know we recovered all the merchandise that was stolen from the murdered lady in Denver."

"Oh, where?"

"In a warehouse on Varick Street. The odd thing is, we don't know who the warehouse belongs to."

"Can't connect it to Ma Mandelbaum?"

"No, she's too smart for that."

"Well," Clint said, "at least she doesn't have Willie to do her dirty work for her anymore."

"And she doesn't have Ben, either."

"What happened?"

"He's gone, disappeared."

Clint thought Ben must have still been wrestling with the guilt he felt, even though it wasn't certain whether it had been his bullets or Willie's that had struck Bethany.

"Well, I guess she won't have Bethany anymore, either, once she gets out of the hospital."

"I doubt any of that will slow Ma down much," Byrnes said.

"I've got to catch my train, Captain," Clint said. "Anything else?"

"Yes," Byrnes said. "The waitress Angie. She asked

me to tell you she's mad at you for not saying a proper good-bye."

He thought he had said a proper good-bye all night the previous night, but he had slipped out this morning without waking her.

"Give her my apologies, will you?"

"Only if you give my best to Roper," Byrnes said in return.

They shook hands again.

"I'm sorry things didn't go . . ." Clint said, then stopped.

"You have your own way of doing things, Mr. Adams," Byrnes said. "Don't we all?"

"Yes, Captain," Clint said, "yes, I guess we do."

Watch for

OUT OF THE PAST

319th novel in the exciting GUNSMITH series
from Jove

Coming in July!

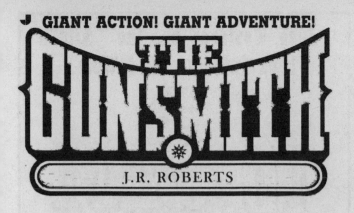

GIANT ACTION! GIANT ADVENTURE!

THE GUNSMITH

J.R. ROBERTS

Little Sureshot And
The Wild West Show
(Gunsmith Giant #9)

Dead Weight
(Gunsmith Giant #10)

Red Mountain
(Gunsmith Giant #11)

The Knights of Misery
(Gunsmith Giant #12)

penguin.com

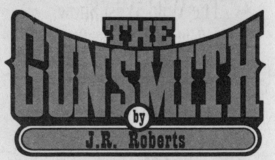